the **oracle** *of* **dating**

the oracle of dating

Allison van Diepen

HARLEQUIN®
TEEN

HARLEQUIN®
TEEN

ISBN-13: 978-0-373-21009-1

THE ORACLE OF DATING

Recycling programs
for this product may
not exist in your area.

To all of the guys I've ever dated.
(Yes, *you*. And even *you*.)

one

New Year's resolutions:

★ Find Tracey a great boyfriend
★ Make a choice about my hair: straight or curly, because wavy just isn't working
★ Cure cereal addiction (possibly through hypnotherapy—see Yellow Pages)
★ Write more blogs for the Oracle of Dating Web site, give lots of dating advice, make stacks of $$$ and quit job at Hellhole
★ Take the Oracle of Dating to the next level!!!

YOU MIGHT THINK that September is a weird time to be making New Year's resolutions. Well, Mom never accused me of doing anything on time, especially tidying my room, loading the dishwasher or Swiffering the kitchen.

"I don't see how you ended up with an eighty average last year, Kayla," Mom says. "You're always chatting online or on the phone."

Which implies that I am not being productive.

The truth is, she has no idea what I'm really up to.

Brrrrinnnggg!

I clear my throat and answer, "The Oracle of Dating."

"It's client number zero-two-four."

"Sabrina?"

"You remember me!"

"I do. What can the Oracle do for you?" I scoot over to my computer and open up my PayPal account to see that her five-dollar payment has been received.

"It's about this guy, Shawn, I'm dating. I hate going out in public with him."

A case of total butt ugly, perhaps?

"Why's that, Sabrina?"

"He always embarrasses me somehow. Like when we went to the school dance Friday night, he was dancing like a maniac. Everybody was staring at him."

"He's a really bad dancer?"

"The worst. It's not just that. Wherever we go, he says

or does something dumb. But when we're alone, he's really sweet!"

"Mmm-hmm." *Listening noises are very important.*

"What do you think I should do?"

"Have you talked to him about this?"

"Yeah, but he doesn't get it."

"I have another question for you, Sabrina. Do you love him?"

"I wouldn't go *that* far. We've only been dating for a couple of months."

"Why not find a guy who wouldn't embarrass you in public?"

"It's not so easy getting a boyfriend. He's only the second one I've ever had."

As I well know. Sabrina's been calling me to discuss every crush and flirtation in the past six months.

"Ask yourself this. Are you with him because you really like him, or because you like having a boyfriend?"

"Er, maybe the second thing."

"How would you feel if he answered the question the same way?"

"I wouldn't like it." She sighs. "I guess I have to break up with him?"

I lift the phone away from my ear and pound a tune into my little xylophone.

"The Oracle has spoken."

"Thank you, Oracle. I know it's the right thing to do."

"Good night, Sabrina."

I KNOW WHAT YOU'RE thinking. What makes me such an expert on dating? Have I had lots of boyfriends?

Um, no.

There have only been two, and both were disasters. But I've learned from each one, and now I think of them, with total detachment, as Case Study No. 1 and Case Study No. 2. I even made retrospective notes.

Case Study No. 1: 9th Grade, November.

Lead-up to relationship: weeks of note-writing and flirting, a subtle ass-grab at a school dance and a kiss behind the portables.

Relationship length: one month.

Activities: playing video games, kissing in his basement, playing more video games.

Conflict: He often wouldn't answer the phone because he didn't want to interrupt his video game. His gaming addiction resulted in a thumb injury for which medical care was required, and he was unable to hold my hand due to a thumb splint.

Outcome: He didn't see me as a girlfriend, he saw me as a gaming partner, make-out buddy and occasional history tutor. So I gave him an ultimatum: "What do you care about more, me or your video games?" He answered: "They're my thing. I'm a gamer, babe." Babe?

Case Study No. 2: 10th Grade, March.

Lead-up to relationship: I met him at a party. He remembered my name and added me on Facebook. We chatted online for a couple of weeks before he finally asked me out.

Conflict: None. He was totally sweet. Or so I thought.

Outcome: After three weeks of going out and making out, he changed his Facebook picture to one of him kissing another girl. ALL of our friends saw this. I called him immediately: "Are you trying to tell me something?" He answered: "Sorry, I didn't know how else to say it."

My two boyfriend disasters only confirmed what I already knew: teenage guys are less mature than teenage girls. Therefore, if I want to date my equal, I should date a guy who is at least twenty, which I would never do, because what sort of twenty-year-old would want to date someone still in high school?

It would've helped a lot to have someone to talk to during those relationships; someone nonjudgmental and anonymous like the Oracle of Dating would have been perfect. I never laugh at a client's concerns or get too preachy. I wish I could've given myself better advice at the time, but it's hard to see clearly when you're emotionally involved.

I decided there was only one solution—to put off dating until college, when the scales of maturity will start to balance. I simply don't have the emotional resilience to deal with immature high school guys. Which isn't to say I wouldn't change my mind if my ideal guy came along, but statistically, it's highly unlikely.

For those teenage girls who are brave enough to deal with teenage guys, and for anyone else who needs me, the Oracle of Dating is there. I do a lot of research so that I can give sensible advice. When I'm not sure of the answers, I tell my clients the Oracle will have to get back to them so that she can "meditate" on their dilemma. My advice is serious, though I've put "for entertainment purposes only" on my Web site so I don't get sued if something I suggest backfires. With all of this responsibility, I don't have time for a love life, anyway.

Besides, I'm not the one who needs a man, my sister does. Tracey is ten years older than I am, and has been coming to me for advice since I was twelve, often trusting my guy radar more than her own. She's even been afraid to introduce certain guys to me because she knows I'll see what she prefers not to see.

Tracey lives on the Upper East Side—it's about forty minutes from Brooklyn by subway. I usually meet her in Manhattan on weekends for lattes, which she insists on paying for. (She says it's fair, considering I don't charge her for advice.) I've also given lots of free advice to her friends. It was actually her best friend, Corinne, who called me the *Oracle* in the first place. After that, the name stuck.

Nothing would make me happier than to find a great match for Tracey. She's an amazing sister, and never makes me feel like a pain when I call her. She's kind, hardworking and selfless—sometimes to a fault—and I won't let her settle for anything less than she deserves. In any other city, she'd have been snatched up by some wonderful guy already, but New York is tricky, since there are far more single women than men, and the dating culture is downright strange. Since she's twenty-six now, I figure she has another few years of trying to find a good man before I'll suggest more extreme measures.

By extreme measures I mean going to Alaska. I see

nothing wrong with that. People move for their careers—why not to find a man? In some parts of Alaska, single men outnumber women ten to one. Tracey would have absolutely no trouble finding a guy there. And I think an Alaskan man—big, strong, not afraid of bugs or heavy lifting—would complement Tracey's personality. The only problem is that she'd be so far away! I guess she'd have to convince her Alaskan man to move to, say, rural Vermont. Because Alaska is just the wrong time zone.

True, there's still a great woman-to-man ratio in the Silicon Valley in California, but I'd prefer she didn't marry a high-tech guy. Dad is in tech, and I don't want Tracey to end up with a guy like him. He and Mom divorced ten years ago, and since then, he's reverted back to the lifestyle he was meant for: the lifestyle of a bachelor. He's traveled the world with his company, living in Singapore, Johannesburg, Berlin and now in Ottawa, Canada. We only see him a couple of times a year, Christmas and summer vacation. And that's fine with me.

I remember the day he left. Mom and Dad sat down with Tracey and me, explaining that he was going to move out. Tracey didn't argue. I think she was sick to death of the fighting. But not me. I thought they should make it work. I used any rationale available to my six-year-old brain to stop them from breaking up. And when none of my arguments worked, I started to cry.

The truth is, Mom and Dad were a disaster from the

start. I'm surprised Mom didn't see through his hollow charm right away, but I guess she was young and innocent, and trusted love. Too bad no one had the guts to stand up at the *speak now or forever hold your peace* part of their wedding, since the only things they had in common— good looks and ridiculous eighties hair—were not enough for a happily ever after.

IT'S A WINDY SUNDAY and I get off the 6 train at Seventy-seventh Street and Lexington to meet Tracey at Starbucks. I see all of the Sunday couples walking around holding hands. Sunday couples are young couples who stay over Saturday night (if you know what I mean) and have carefully assembled designer sweats, sneakers and baseball caps to wear on Sundays. They always look freshly showered and slightly hungover and you find them ordering greasy breakfasts at Second Avenue diners before spending their afternoons browsing shops, buying artwork for their tiny apartments and crowding neighborhood cafés so that I can hardly ever get a seat.

Tracey is looking beautiful today, though she has puffiness under her eyes, indicating that she either slept too little or too much. She has rich dark hair the color of a flourless chocolate cake and shining brown eyes to match. Her cheeks are slightly pink from the windy day, and her complexion is flawless. At five-nine, she's four inches taller than me, giving a sleek elegance to her figure that many girls would kill for.

As for me, I've inherited my dad's Shredded Wheat–colored hair and my mom's hazel eyes, which are mistaken for green or brown depending on the day, light conditions and my mood.

Today Tracey is wearing fresh unscuffed New Balance sneakers. Sunday is the only day of the week you won't find her in heels of at least two inches—an error in judgment, IMO, since it tends to narrow her pool of possible guys to those five-eleven and above. But I guess that's her choice, her preference being men over six feet—not always easy to find unless you're in Denmark or Norway.

She gives me a big hug and two European cheek kisses, and I know I'll have to take my compact out to see what lipstick smudges she left.

At the counter, we're served by a skinny guy we privately nicknamed Pip. He's there every weekend and talks like Mickey Mouse.

"Tall soy iced Tazo chai latte," he says to the huge guy behind the espresso machine.

"Tall soy iced Tazo chai latte," the huge guy repeats in a booming voice.

"Uh, no foam, please," Tracey adds.

Pip turns to me. "Miss?"

"I'll have a tall soy latte." (Lactose intolerance runs in the family, if you haven't guessed.)

We find a little table on the upper level in the midst of several twentysomethings on laptops. An old man is dozing in one of the comfy chairs, his mouth hanging open. I angle my seat so I don't have to see if a fly swoops in there.

"Did you go out last night?" I ask.

Her lips spread in a smile. "It was awesome."

"Tell me, tell me!"

She giggles. "His name's Miguel."

"Your salsa instructor?"

"Yes. We had drinks at Bar Nine. He was telling me that he does an hour and a half of yoga a day—talk about self-discipline! Anyway, after drinks we went to a salsa bar. I was stepping all over his feet, and I actually got super-dizzy when he spun me around, but I didn't want to tell him that." She leans closer to me and lowers her voice. "It was so hot."

I raise my eyebrows.

"I know what you're thinking, Kayla. You're thinking that a salsa instructor is obviously sleeping with half his students. But he's not like that at all. In fact, he won't even give bachata lessons—it's too personal."

"I think he sounds fab."

She blinks. "You do?"

"Sure, I do." I sip my latte. "I only have one piece of advice."

"Uh-oh."

"Don't sleep with him for at least a month."

"I *knew* you were going to say that."

Tracey and I are pretty open about her sex life. (Well,

the fact that she *has* one.) She promised to tell me everything I want to know if I agreed to stay a virgin until I
was at least eighteen. I told her we had a deal. I didn't plan
on having another boyfriend before then, anyway.

"How's business?" she asks.

"It's good. Look what I've got." I open my knapsack
and pull out a bunch of business cards.

She examines one. "This is fantastic! How'd you do this?"

"I just did it on Word. It's easy. I got the card stock
from Staples."

"Can I have a few? Maybe I can get you some business.
A lot of my colleagues need a service like this."

I give her a stack. "I have hundreds."

She puts them in her purse. "Maybe I'll ask for a com-
mission. Say, ten percent?" She winks.

"How's work going, anyway?"

"Ugh, it's a gong show! We're supposed to deliver this
software to clients at the end of the month and we're running into all these obstacles we didn't expect."

That's another thing about my sister. She speaks an alien
language known only to Gen Y guys in square-rimmed
glasses: the language of computers. She's a software de-
veloper for a company called Hexagon. Unfortunately, I
don't share her smarts in technical stuff. But I can blog
easily, and only need her help for the Web site design.

"You won't guess who's back working in the office,"
she says.

Uh-oh. Don't say it. "Scott."

"Yep. And he had the nerve to ask if I wanted to go out for drinks with him and Matt and Chris on Friday. I told him, *'Sorry, I have plans.'* Can you believe that guy?"

I can. It's Scott's style. He was her boyfriend for seven months only to end it with "I'm not sure if I'm ready for a full-blown relationship." As if it were a disease.

Yes, they were once one of those Upper East Side Sunday couples.

But Scott hadn't stopped with dumping her. That would be too quick and easy. Over the next few months he kept calling, pretending he was confused, tortured. And in spite of my warning to ignore his calls, she always answered them, hoping that he'd want something real.

His calls faded, eventually.

But now he's back.

Intelligent woman that she is, I should be sure that she won't give that loser the time of day, right?

Wrong. Tracey doesn't always have the best judgment when it comes to dating, which is why it's so important that I weigh in. I always wondered if Tracey was messed up by my parents' marriage (not by their divorce—*that* was the healthy part). She was sixteen when it happened, and it sent her skidding off in the wrong direction—grades sliding, bad boyfriends, borderline eating disorder. Thank God Mom managed to get her back on track, but I wonder if the scars remain. Is she destined to be attracted to unreliable types like our dad?

"Don't you dare, Tracey."

"I won't. What, you think I'm stupid?"

That's the thing about being the Oracle. Sometimes you know things you don't want to know.

I USED TO THINK SUNDAY nights sucked because the excitement of the weekend is over and a whole week of waking up early stretches ahead of me. Plus, ever since Mom gave me the choice of whether or not to go to church, I usually sleep until noon, so I can never get to sleep at a good time.

When I realized that my friends were going through the same Sunday-night blues, I decided to take action and organize a weekly get-together. And now, Sunday night embodies everything we love (to hate): the rich bitches, the beautiful people, the trash-talkers, the sex-crazed and the backstabbers. In other words, *Glamour Girl*. Or, as Mom calls it, potato chips for your brain—they taste good but have no nutritional value.

We're in Viv's basement on beanbag chairs in front of the flat-screen TV, except for Amy, who is stretched out luxuriantly on the sofa in her *Don't Feed the Models* tee.

On the coffee table is an assortment of traditional East Indian faves: samosas, pakoras, badgies. It's one of the things I look forward to about our Sunday nights here.

"Your mom is such a great cook!"

Viv gives me a funny look. "These are from Costco."

"Oh." I suppose it makes sense. Her mom is a doctor at New York Presbyterian and hardly has time to make us food.

Viv's parents are strict and traditional and from the same part of India as Gandhi. Her parents are too innocent themselves to know what this *Glamour Girl* business is all about. That, plus Viv's quick reflexes with the PVR, makes it possible for us to watch the show here in the first place.

Poor Viv will never even admit to being attracted to a guy who isn't Indian, and there are only about five Indian guys at our entire school. I suppose that gives her an excuse for not having a boyfriend—an excuse the rest of us don't have.

Well, maybe I shouldn't include Amy in the not-having-a-boyfriend category. Amy is a blue-eyed blonde, very good-looking, and knows it. She calls Chad her boyfriend, but we all know that he's a MOB (make-out buddy). I'm not knocking it. Although the Oracle would say such relationships aren't emotionally healthy, there's a certain practicality in them. I mean, she's horny as hell, and so is he. And while he's a little simple, he has cute dimples and a soccer bod.

I'm munching on a samosa when Viv pauses the show. Amy curses. "But it was just getting hot!"

Sharese smacks her knee. "They're finally gonna do it!"

Ryan grunts his agreement, hairpins in his mouth. He is braiding Sharese's hair. She always complained that no white person could do a good job with it, but Ryan has proved her wrong.

Viv says, "I was just thinking—what would the Oracle of Dating say about this? I mean, isn't Harrison obviously just using her?"

Everybody groans.

Amy rolls her eyes. "The Oracle is full of it! It's just somebody making a quick buck. Don't buy into it."

"The Oracle didn't make any money off *me*," Viv insists. "I just read her blog."

I stuff another samosa into my mouth.

"I bet the Oracle is some fifty-year-old businessman trying to exploit us," Sharese says.

Viv shakes her head. "I think you're wrong. She's definitely female, and she knows what she's talking about."

Way to go, Viv! She is my sole defender in a sea of haters.

You really can't blame me for keeping my true identity from my friends. I love them, but I know that being the Oracle of Dating would make me the object of constant teasing. I need one thing that's safe, and just mine.

two

"MICHAELA, WHAT DO YOU THINK?"

I snap to attention. Practice kicks in. Instead of saying, "Huh?" I say, "Sorry, I'm not sure I understand the question."

Ms. Goff starts to reword it, but stops when she hears a choked laugh from the seat across from me. "Something funny, Jared?"

"Nope." He squelches a smile.

Ms. Goff goes back to her question, and I manage to answer it, taking the heat off. But as soon as she turns back to the board, I shoot the guy an *I don't appreciate you laughing at me* glare.

He turns his head and looks directly at me, blue eyes crinkling at the corners with amusement.

Oh, I get it. He's onto my little strategy.

Jared Stewart is a snob if I ever saw one. He doesn't so-cialize with many people, and it's not in a shy, sweet kind of way, but in a *why bother* way—I can tell the difference. Worse, he's totally good-looking in an *I don't care* sort of way; I'm talking messy almost-black hair, careless clothes and torn-up shoes, obviously vintage. He's lean, but muscular lean, not coked-up rock-star lean, and he's got big hands, and feet that have to be at least a size thirteen…and why am I thinking about this?

The bell rings. Well, it's not actually a bell, it's a ding-dong over the P.A. system. Speaking of Ding Dongs, thank God it's lunchtime. By this time every day I'm so hungry I'm ready to play *Survivor* and chew the bark off a desk leg. Not that the lunch menu in the caf is much better.

I pick up my books and walk out, sensing Jared behind me. In the hall, he touches my arm, says something. I notice he's got a red spot on his chin like he shaved over a zit this morning. I can't help but think that shaving is sexy—that it separates the men from the boys.

I realize I'm not listening to him. "What?"

"I said don't take it personally, all right?"

"Uh, okay."

And he walks off.

I make my way to the caf, where Sharese and Viv are in line getting food and Ryan is already at our end of the table, playing solitaire.

Amy has a different lunch period. Sadly, the office doesn't accommodate cliques. Not that we're much of one. Anyone can hang around with us if they want. But if you're totally into chess or computers, you probably won't. And if you're really popular, you won't, either. But anyone is welcome.

After getting my lunch, I join my friends at the table. "Who's winning?" I ask Ryan, whose head is bent over the cards.

He snorts. "You working tonight?"

"Five to nine. You?"

"Four to eight."

Just the thought of Eddie's Grocery (aka the Hellhole) fills me with dread. If only being the Oracle of Dating paid more, it could be my only job. I scan the cafeteria. So many potential clients! I could make a fortune on the Chess Club alone.

I take a few bites of the caf's low-fat pizza. It tastes like cardboard. "So, what's the status of Operation Dairy Freez?"

"Shh." Sharese looks around conspiratorially. "Honestly, I don't know what to do about it."

"We'll kidnap him," Ryan says. "You can have your way with him in the back of my parents' SUV."

We giggle.

"Has anyone found out his last name?" Viv asks.

We shake our heads. We know him only as Mike P., or the future father of Sharese's children.

All we really know about him is that he works at the Dairy Freez ice-cream shop on DeKalb Avenue, and that he's tall and gangly, with big, kind eyes. Also, he has good customer-service skills. Like when that fat guy's third scoop fell off his cone, Mike P. not only replaced the scoop, but apologized for not pressing it down hard enough the first time.

We've already given Sharese and Mike P. our blessing. The problem is, they still haven't gotten past the "Hi, can I take your order?" stage.

"Stop putting pressure on me, guys. You're making me nervous." So far, Sharese has been too shy to do anything about Mike P. But we're all hoping that will change.

Of course, like with anything, she can't be sure he's interested. Sharese is hot, in a voluptuous, full-figured way, and we've spotted Mike P. glancing at her chest—always a good sign. Plus, he gets extra shy when she comes up—another good sign. But as for a guy's tastes, you never really know.

"It's about time you took a risk," I tell her.

"What about you, Kayla?" Sharese fires back. "Since when do you take risks?"

"I don't have a crush on anyone." Which is true. Which isn't to say I'm not *attracted* to anyone. I'm not immune to Jared, for instance. And who can blame me, since it's universally known that dark, mysterious guys are attractive, especially when they have big hands that I'm sure could crush a Coke can with a single squeeze.

Okay, it's obvious that, like my friends, I have my fair share of hormonal urges. I just have the presence of mind not to take them seriously.

Ryan touches my hair. "You could get any guy you want if you did something with your hair. This wash-and-go thing isn't working for you."

I tug on a lock self-consciously. He's right, of course. My hair is neither straight nor curly, but has a drunken wave. I can't tame it with a blow-dryer, so my only other option is a professional-strength straightening iron, but the idea of putting something so hot near my head worries me.

"You should get highlights, too," Ryan says. "Café au lait is a good color for you. And you should wear a skirt for a change and show off your legs."

"I'll keep that in mind." Last year I made the mistake of letting Ryan take me shopping with my birthday money. I came home with an outfit that made me look like a high-class escort, complete with a sheer blouse, short skirt and tall leather boots. All promptly returned the next day when my mom had a conniption.

"You're such a fake," Sharese says. "You're really not interested in *anyone*? Not even Declan McCall?"

Why is Declan McCall, football MVP and ex-boyfriend of ice queen Brooke Crossley, our school's default crush? "Declan doesn't turn me on. Whenever I've talked to him, all he does is stare at my chest. And I don't even have a chest."

My friends can't argue with that.

"Well, Brooke got what she deserved when he dumped her on her pretty ass," Ryan says.

Yes, though I've never seen it, I bet Brooke Crossley has

a pretty ass. She has a pretty everything else and everyone loves to hate her for it. But I doubt she's as terrible as they say. Sure, she's snobby, but a lot of people are. And she isn't an airhead, either. Not that she's as good a student as I am—but she can't have everything, can she?

As I munch on tasteless pizza, I wonder if Brooke is a possible client. Maybe she needs to talk to someone about her recent breakup. I'll have to drop a business card in her locker.

WHEN I GET HOME from work that night, I turn my attention to the topic of breakups. Why would someone like Declan McCall break up with Brooke Crossley when she's clearly the best match for him at school? They could've been voted Prom King and Queen next year if they'd stayed together. I wonder if he got bored with her, or if there were other factors involved.

Seems to me that my female clients are more forgiving of their boyfriends' flaws than the other way around. But there are some good reasons to cut a guy loose…

Top Ten Reasons
You Should Cut Him Loose

10. When you're kissing him, you're fantasizing about someone else (like his best friend)!

9. You're only with him because you want to have a boyfriend.

8. He tells you he doesn't want a relationship. Believe him—he doesn't!

7. He makes hurtful comments like, "Easy on the fries, honey."

6. He doesn't show affection in public. It doesn't need to be a lot, but if he won't even hold your hand, he wants people to think he's single!

5. He gives you a promise ring in the first two months. Puh-lease!

4. He gives you a cell phone or a pager so that he can keep track of you.

3. He ogles other girls in front of you. Think of what he's doing behind your back!

2. Finishing a level of his favorite video game is more important than answering your phone call.

1. He says, "Baby, if you loved me, you'd..." Anything starting with that is a manipulation! Don't fall for it!

THE NEXT BIZARRO REALITY TV show should be all about _my_ life. All I need to round out the cast is a washed-up child star and a slutty _Survivor_ castoff.

My mom is a minister, for God's sake. She's got the threads (the robe and the stole), the cross around her neck and the travel-size Communion set.

Allison van Diepen

Mom works at a church in Park Slope where she, among other things, performs gay commitment ceremonies and doesn't make couples who are living together feel guilty. She also preaches about the gift of divorce as the congregation nods in agreement. She says her divorce is the best thing that ever happened to her, next to having her children, of course. If she hadn't gotten a divorce, she wouldn't be so happy in her career and she wouldn't have met her new husband, Erland.

Now, Mom and I have different views on the merits of the Swede. She would say that he is a brilliant theology professor and that they have a meeting of minds. I would say that he is way too stuffy and has no idea how to deal with young people. The guy has a thick accent, not unlike the Swedish chef, and is nine years older than she is—definitely a second-round draft pick. But that's what happens when you make the wrong choice the first time around.

Mom met the Swede two years ago at a theological conference in Atlanta where he delivered a paper called, "The Existential and Metaphysical Legacy of Martin Luther." Doesn't that just scream romance?

Mom came back from the conference all giddy, which was cool because she had been single, way single, for a long time. So they embarked on a long-distance relationship with frequent trips overseas and endless hours on the phone. Which is, incidentally, when I successfully petitioned for my own phone line, which I now use for the Oracle.

It was all going great for a while. Mom was happy. I was happy that Mom was happy. And the Swede wasn't much of a bother, since he'd stop in when he was in town but never spend the night at our place. But then, last year, the Swede announced that he got a job at Union Theological Seminary in Manhattan, and within a couple of months they were married and he'd set up shop in her bedroom.

The Swede does not look like a Swede should (like a Ken doll). He is about five-nine, stocky, and has red hair that has been taken over by gray. For which I would suggest Just for Men, but I doubt it carries his particular copper-red color, and even if it did, I doubt he would use it, considering the way he lets his eyebrows go.

Today at breakfast, when Mom comes in, the Swede says, "Good morning, Bunny."

Bunny? I hope he means it like Honey Bunny instead of Playboy Bunny.

The Swede + Mom + Sex = SO WRONG.

I've never actually heard them having sex, thank God, but I'm pretty sure that's why Mom asks me about my social plans—so she and the Swede can cozy it up in their king-size love boat, drunk on endless cups of Earl Grey.

"Morning, honey." Mom kisses him on the lips. Then she comes over to me and kisses the top of my head. "Morning, sweetie."

Breakfast is a mostly silent thing. And that's fine, because Mom and I are not morning people, and the Swede is not one for light conversation. So as we eat, we read. Mom is reading the *Methodist Church Observer,* the Swede is reading *Theology Today,* and I am reading *Teen People.*

I'm seeing all these articles with gorgeous, airbrushed girls, and I say to Mom, "I'm an eight out of ten, right? Looks-wise?"

"You're the same as I was at your age."

"What does that mean?"

"It's a good thing."

"Uh…" Can't she just be like other moms and tell me what I want to hear?

"You really shouldn't spend your time thinking about these things. Don't try to conform to a media-created rating scale."

See what I mean? A simple question becomes a sermon. I'm not saying she doesn't have a point, but can't she humor me?

Maybe I'm wrong about living in a reality show. Maybe I'm living in a sitcom. The audience is laughing, but I'm not getting paid.

Now, I don't want to give the impression that the Oracle of Dating is getting hundreds of phone calls, instant messages and e-mails a week. My average is two contacts per night.

The Web site color scheme is pink and blue, symbol-izing guys and girls. Instead of headings at the top, Tracey created bubbles, which include: About the Oracle; Contact the Oracle; Blog; Links. In the center of the homepage is a large box for a blog that I can update myself. I also post a Q and A of the week, and allow readers to comment.

I like my Web site to be as interactive as possible, so I put up a new poll once a week. This week's is, *If you were stranded on a desert island with one celebrity hottie, who would it be?* Next week's will be, *What's your all-time favorite romantic movie?* Other times I create a quiz to test my readers' knowledge of relationships. Widgets of all kinds can be found for free, so polls and quizzes are easy to do. The key is to have a site that people will keep coming back to. Static content won't do. The average reader visits the site several times before asking me a question, so I need to keep them returning.

If I'm online, the Oracle icon will be lit up. Customers wanting to instant message me can click on the icon and five dollars will be deducted from their PayPal account for the first twenty minutes. At first I'd thought using PayPal would be too complicated, but Tracey said it's just a matter of putting the payment button on my page and allowing PayPal to take a small percentage off each transaction. I figured it was worth it, not only because it's easy, but because several customers had stiffed me through the mail.

The worst is when these random guys call to ask "sexual questions." Usually that's just a cover for something else. So one night I ask, "Why don't you call one of those 1-900 sex lines?" And the guy replies, "'Cause they're a helluva lot more expensive. Anyway, you sound young. I like that."

I slam down the phone and write down his number for the list of psycho-perverts whose calls I have to block.

When the phone rings again, it's just after nine p.m.

I answer, "The Oracle."

"Okay, so I have this question."

"First, is there a name I can call you? It doesn't have to be your real name. Whatever you're comfortable with." I check my PayPal account and see that the payment's been received.

"Call me Melanie."

"All right, Melanie. Go ahead with your question."

"There's this boy I like. His family is friends with my family. We even live on the same street. We used to hang out together all the time. But he hasn't paid me any attention in the past few months. He really hurt me."

"How old are you, Melanie?"

"Fourteen."

I get this type of call a lot. Girls often find their guy friends drifting away when they enter their teenage years. There's really no way to prevent it.

"The truth is, at your age, guys usually like to spend most of their time with other guys."

"But what about me?"

"I'm not saying he doesn't like you anymore. He might be going through puberty as we speak, and he could be uncomfortable around girls."

"He talks to girls, just not me. He's starting to hang around with the popular crowd now—all the kids he used to hate."

"It sounds like he's trying to adjust socially. I know this is sad for you, but he needs to find himself."

"How do I get him back?"

"Are you willing to do whatever it takes?"

"Yeah, anything."

I play a few notes on the xylophone. "The Oracle believes that you'll have to wait, Melanie. Give him time with these other friends. Don't guilt-trip him. Hopefully he'll realize what a great friend you are and come back to you."

"How long will it take?"

"It could be months, or years. But once he's more comfortable with his place in the world, he'll probably wonder what happened to your friendship. And Melanie, I think this is for the best. So give him time…and the Oracle has a good instinct that he will come around."

"Okay, I'll try to be patient. But it's hard."

"The Oracle never said life was easy."

"I understand. Thanks, Oracle."

"You're welcome, Melanie."

ART CLASS. Have this cool young teacher, Ms. Gerstad, who wears a skirt over her jeans—totally cool but I'd never have the nerve to go *that* hippy. Gerstad lives the artsy life and isn't shy to tell us about it. She spends every Wednesday night watching or performing in the Poetry Slam at the Nuyorican Café in the East Village. The rest of her time is divided between vegan cafés and anarchist bookstores.

Today she tells us that our First Marking Period project is to draw people. Great. I'd prefer to splash paint all over the page like a kindergartener and call it abstract art. I only took this class because I need an art credit and both drama and dance conflicted with my schedule.

She gives us some magazines to inspire us, though tracing, unfortunately, is forbidden. Then she reminds us that we'll be able to see examples of portraiture a week from Friday on our field trip to the Museum of Modern Art. She seems to think viewing the works of the greats will inspire us. I wonder how she'll react if I pull a Picasso and draw people's arms sticking out of their heads.

"Who did you choose?" It's Lauren, my art-class friend, looking over my shoulder. "I'm doing Jessica Biel."

I bet lots of people are doing Jessica Biel. Her face and figure are total perfection and her teeth would make a cosmetic dentist proud.

But perfection is no fun. Not for me, anyway.

"Got any other magazines at your table?" I ask her. "I just have *Cosmo* and *Elle.*"

"Sure, come see."

I go to her table, which today she's sharing with Jared Stewart. He doesn't look up, he's working too hard. His sleeves are rolled up and I notice veins bulging in his forearms as he sketches. I look a little closer. His sketch is amazing. He's drawing an old man sitting on a stoop in Latin America. The picture is from the *National Geographic* open in front of him.

"Uh, sorry, can I see that magazine?" I ask.

He looks up. "Yeah." He rips out the picture he's working on and hands me the magazine.

I flip through it with Lauren. In the corner of my vision, I see that his hand is now poised above the sketch like he doesn't know what to do next. His brows are frowning, his mouth tight, and his hand's gripping the pencil as if he's about to strike the page. *A tortured artist,* I can't help but think. *A hot, deliciously tortured artist.* Then I give my head a shake, berate myself silently and focus back on the task at hand.

"What about that one?" Lauren points to a picture of a toddler on a beach. It's cute but I know it's not the one. There's nothing in this magazine. As I close it, I see *the* picture on the cover.

"I'm doing this!"

I've seen this photograph before. It's of an Afghan girl with piercing green eyes.

Jared glances at the picture and mutters, "Good luck with that."

Could he be any more sarcastic? Lauren and I look at each other and shrug. I take the magazine back to my desk and get to work.

I start a sketch. Halfway through, I realize it looks like a *Simpsons* character, so I crumple it up and start again. I'm going to start with her face, then do the burka after.

I'll never get an A on this. Maybe a D or a C if I'm lucky. My average will plummet, I'll never get into college, and I'll end up working at the Hellhole for the rest of my life. Maybe one day I'll be manager, marry Jay the stoner, Afrim the meat man or Juan the stock boy, and my kids will grow up running the aisles. My breath escapes in a sigh. Jared must've heard it, because he comes up beside me. "How's it going?"

Instinctively, my hands cover my drawing.

His mouth crooks. "Not so good, then?"

I reveal the sketch, daring a glance at him. "I'm not an artist."

He frowns. "I see what you mean."

My mouth drops open. He so didn't say that!

"Well, you've got a few weeks to do something better," he says.

"Are you going to help me?"

He leans against my desk, crossing his arms. "Are you going to pay me?"

"Yeah, right."

"Fine. I'll help you, anyway, if you don't piss me off in the meantime."

From any other person, I'd think it was a joke, but I'm not sure about Jared Stewart. He's a cynic if there ever was one.

I meet his eyes. "More likely *you* would piss *me* off."

The corner of his mouth twitches. I can tell he likes my answer.

SOME OF MY CLIENTS complain that they don't know how to flirt, or they can't recognize when someone is flirting with them. I can relate. Like today, I'm pretty sure Jared Stewart flirted with me, if only for a split-second. Or was I the one flirting with him? All I know is, I'm wasting far too much time thinking about it.

Time for a little flirting 101.

How to Flirt

The art of flirting is only perfected through practice. Your key tools are your smile and your eyes. First, walk into the room projecting openness and confidence, your lips turned up a little as if you're pleased to be there. People notice others who are cheerful and gravitate toward them.

Allison van Diepen

Scan the area for hotties. Don't immediately focus on just one unless, unfortunately, there is just one in the whole room. (If so, you should find another party!) Try to catch his eye. When you do, look for two full seconds, smile and look away. There, you've been officially noticed. Talk to your friends, laugh and have a good time, and occasionally scan the vicinity to see if he's looking your way. If so, make eye contact again.

Find a way to get closer to him. If he's on the dance floor, it's pretty easy. Just dance in his direction, keep up the eye contact and you'll be dancing together in no time. If the object of your attraction isn't on the dance floor, find a way to move to his end of the room without being too obvious. If he is standing near the bar/refreshment table, go up to get a drink—don't bring a friend because that will make it difficult for him to talk to you. Look around and be approachable. Give him a smile and say hi.

When you start talking, it doesn't matter what you say as much as how you say it. It's okay if the conversation is a little mundane at first ("Crowded in here, huh?") as long as you're interacting. Go with the flow of the conversation—hopefully it will lead to something interesting after the initial awkwardness. Use body language to show your interest—nod at appropriate times, react to what he's saying, touch his forearm if you can fit it in naturally...

You can take it from there. Good luck!

The Oracle

three

"Eek!" I yank my foot out of the whirling footbath.

The Chinese lady giving me the pedicure smiles. "Yo' feet sensitive."

Viv giggles. "Aren't you used to it by now, Kayla?"

I twitch as the lady scrubs my foot. "I'll never be."

Oh, the price of vanity. Well, despite my ticklishness problem, this fifteen-dollar mani and pedi can't be beat.

I look over at Viv. She has shoulder-length black hair with the healthy bounce of a Nutrisse model. Her best feature is her wide-set liquid-black eyes and thick dark lashes that don't even need mascara. She's so pretty, and she hasn't even kissed a guy. What a travesty!

It's all her parents' fault. They forbid her to even think about going out with a guy who isn't Indian. Problem is, the only Indian guy Viv was ever interested in moved away last year, leaving her prospects martini dry. (I love that expression. Tracey's friend Corinne uses it all the time to refer to her hair or her bank account.)

Enter Max McIver, a cute guy with spiky brown hair who's in her A.P. History class. It's obvious to everyone that they're into each other and that they'd make the perfect couple. He seems mature for his age, so I think he's a good bet for Viv's first relationship. Funny and easygoing, Max is just the right candidate to show our beloved Viv a good time.

"I saw you and Max flirting in the hall today. He's cute, don't you think?"

She glares at me. Whoa, venom! It's total proof that she's hiding her affection for him.

"He's just a friend. I'm not interested."

"Come on, Viv. I won't tell anyone."

"I know. But I don't want him, Kayla. You know I only like brown boys."

I wonder if she's saying that to remind me or to convince herself. Either way, I'm not going to argue.

She turns to me. "Do you think Ryan is gay?"

"Where'd that come from?"

"Everybody's saying he is."

"He says he isn't."

"But, Kayla, he wants to be a fashion designer! My brother says that's totally gay."

The Chinese woman doing my feet sputters on laughter and starts talking a mile a minute with the woman doing Viv's feet. Are they laughing at our conversation? I'll never know.

"Ryan says he isn't gay, Viv. I didn't ask him—one day he just said it. So I believe him."

"All right. I believe him, too."

"And does it matter if he is? I mean, who cares? My mom will do his wedding either way."

When the pedicures are finished, we waddle over to the other end of the salon in our flip-flops and sit down for manicures. Viv decides to make her nails a shade lighter than her pedicure. My color-of-the-season is guava and I remain faithful.

"Hopefully our nails will last until your birthday," she says.

My birthday is on September 27th, two weeks and two days away, not that I'm counting. "I doubt the mani will last, but I can always come back for a touch-up."

"You may have to. Ryan is planning your birthday and he says we all have to look our best. He says it's a requirement."

"That's hilarious. I can't wait."

"Any gift requests?"

"Oh, come on. You know I don't want anything."

"You come on. As if we won't get you anything."

It's a good point. We're pretty good gift givers in our group. Our gifts aren't expensive, but they're always creative.

"I can't believe we're getting all these assignments already," she says.

"You'll do great. You always do."

"Probably, but I hate working so hard."

Her parents are hard-core. They go to parent-teacher conferences demanding the dates of all the tests so they know when to keep Viv at home studying.

"At least *you* have some easy classes like art," she says.

I laugh because it's so ironic. "Easy, maybe, if I had some talent. It'll probably be my worst mark. Have you thought about your sociology paper yet? It's a quarter of our final mark."

"I'm almost done."

"You're unbelievable! What's it on?"

"How patients relate to their doctors."

"Good idea. I'm actually thinking of doing a dating experiment. Have you heard of speed dating?"

She nods.

"I want to organize a speed-dating night at my place. Thought it might be fun to observe it and write a paper on it."

"That's an amazing idea!"

"I was hoping you'd volunteer to be one of the speed daters. I need ten girls and ten guys. Will you do it?"

"Will there be any Indian guys?"

"I promise to try to get some."

"Okay, then. Count me in!"

THAT EVENING TRACEY calls to tell me about her date with the salsa instructor.

She has a fantastic dinner with Miguel at a Cuban

restaurant in the Village. She leaves the restaurant on his arm, drunk on wine and their fiery attraction. He takes her to his favorite club, Calienté. Music pumps hot and fierce. He brings her onto the dance floor and leads her in a passionate set.

"You're on fire," he says. "You make love to me with your moves."

Tracey feels vibrant and alive. She pictures herself dancing the merengue in her wedding dress as her friends and family look on in awe. Maybe one day she and Miguel will open up their own dance school. Maybe they'll spend their summers teaching underprivileged children salsa in the streets of Guadalajara.

After a while she pleads exhaustion and takes a breather. At the bar, she orders a mojito, extra sugar. She'll need the energy for the night of dancing ahead.

Miguel is now dancing with another woman. This is typical at salsa clubs—everybody dances with everybody. She doesn't mind. The girl he's chosen is a tentative dancer and heavy-set. He is apparently giving her instruction, and she is trying very hard not to step on his toes.

Tracey gulps down her drink, eager to get back. But when the next song comes on, he's already found another partner. Tracey's jaw drops when she sees that he's dancing with a gorgeous Latina in a skin-tight white minidress.

The beat of the music is distinctive. It's the bachata!

Doesn't he only dance that with special people? Isn't it too personal?

Tracey watches as they tear up the dance floor. It's the most extraordinary dance she's ever seen—and if this guy weren't *her* date, she'd be enthralled.

A woman sitting beside her mutters in a smoker's voice, "Those two should get a room."

At that moment Tracey becomes aware of several things:

She will never be able to rival a full-blooded Latina on the dance floor.

She will never be able to stand the jealousy of knowing that Miguel makes love to countless women in the form of Latin dancing.

Miguel is a gift to women everywhere. A Casanova. A bird not meant to be caged.

Tracey slaps down a ten for her drink. "Who was I kidding?" And leaves.

THIS IS RIDICULOUS. I have an awesome Web site that only a couple of hundred people know about. I need thousands, not hundreds, to make a splash.

I have to advertise.

I spend my entire Saturday making up a colorful, catchy flyer, then I go to Kinko's to make copies. I put up about thirty in malls and subway stations. Too bad I can't ask my friends to help with my advertising blitz, but it isn't worth giving up my anonymity.

That night I sit in front of my computer. So far I've gotten fifteen hits. That's not bad. I'm hoping someone will IM me. Instead, the Oracle's phone line rings.

"The Oracle of Dating."

"Hi. I saw your Web site. I have, ah, an issue that I'm dealing with."

"You can count on me for unbiased advice." My words are smooth, but excitement bubbles inside me. The woman on the phone sounds twenty-five or thirty—that means my advertisements are finally helping me reach a different age group!

"You sound really young," she says.

Uh-oh, what do I say to that? *Think, Oracle, think.*

"Would you prefer a fresh voice, or a jaded one?"

She laughs. "Good answer. Here goes. I went onto a dating site and started chatting with a few guys. I ended up making dates with two in the same week. And the thing is, I liked both of them. I figured I'd go on a few dates with each of them and eventually one or both would fade out. But it didn't happen that way. It's been a month and I'm still dating them."

"Do you prefer one to the other?"

"No, I'm crazy about both of them! They're just so different. One is reserved and straitlaced—but still waters run deep, you know. And the other is exciting and passionate and even wants to meet my parents."

"Are you being intimate with either of them?"

"I, ah, fooled around with both of them. I feel guilty about it, but I can't seem to stop myself. It's like the guilt is an aphrodisiac. Does that make sense?"

"It does, yes. Tell me, do these guys know you're dating other people?"

"I don't think so. At the beginning, I told them I wasn't looking to be exclusive right away, but they both think that I've changed my mind. One of them is even calling me his girlfriend."

"Do you want an exclusive relationship?"

"Yes, I just don't know who I want it with! What if I choose one of them and it doesn't work out? Then I've let go of the other guy for nothing."

"I have one last question for you before I give my advice. How would you feel if you were in the position of these men?"

"I'd feel like I was being played. And that's not how I want them to feel. I don't want to hurt anyone."

"Thank you for your honesty. Now, here is my advice…" I hit a few notes on the xylophone.

"What was *that*?"

"A xylophone."

"That's weird! Okay, Oracle of Dating, so what's your advice?"

"My advice is that you spend the next two weeks dating these guys as if you're interviewing them for a job—the job is being your boyfriend. Take everything into account—reliability, fun factor, physical attraction. Make a list if you have to. At the end of two weeks, make your decision. Be as nice as possible to the other guy—explain to him that this isn't a good time for you to embark on a relationship, but you want to remain friends. If it's a relatively good breakup, he might consider letting you back into his life in the future."

"You're so right, Oracle. Thank you. I'm going to take your advice." She pauses. "One last question—how old are you, anyway?"

"The Oracle is timeless."

"You're funny. I like that. Have a good night."

"You, too. And good luck."

"PRICE CHECK, CASH TWO!"

There are four cash registers in the whole store and mine is the only one that's open. Ryan left a while ago, and the other cashier, Jay, is probably smoking a spliff in the back room.

"Price check!" I repeat, feeling the customer glaring at me.

The stock boys loading up the shelves in aisle one pretend they don't understand English.

"Juan!" He finally looks up. "Check this, okay?" I hold up the bag of chips. "Find out if they're on sale."

"*Sì.*" He runs toward the chip aisle.

He's back a couple of minutes later with another bag. "This. Not that."

The customer chose Baked Lays instead of regular Lays.
A common mistake.

"Do you still want them?" I ask.

She makes a face. "For three forty-nine? Are you crazy?"

"Sometimes I think I'm heading there," I mumble.

"Did you talk back to me?"

"Huh? Me? No."

"Good!"

I scan the rest of her groceries, pack them and total it
up. After I count back her change, she counts it again carefully, like she's sure I shortchanged her. Then she picks up
her bags and leaves.

Little does she know that I arranged for her canned
goods to squash her bread. Ha! It's a hollow revenge,
really. But it's all I've got.

Work is high up on my list of the worst places in the
world to be, next to a holiday in Iraq or a hiking trip in
the mountains of Afghanistan. Since my Web site is getting more hits these days, I hope my days of working here
are numbered.

Mom thinks this job is teaching me a work ethic. It definitely is, but not the one she had in mind.

Everybody at Eddie's Grocery is corrupt, from the
price-gouging store manager to the cashiers and stock
boys who give themselves five-finger discounts. My co-
workers actually think I'm weird because I don't steal. I

tell them it's nothing against them, I just have an unfortunate Christian morality complex.

Every single person at this store hates their job except
Petie, a twenty-year-old with Down syndrome who helps
out in the bakery. I think the manager actually gets
money from some Community Living program to let
Petie work here. It's unbelievable, really. We should be
paying Petie for being the only person to walk in with a
smile on his face.

One time I dropped a comment in the Customers'
Views box. Instead of playing horrid elevator music, I
suggested that we play motivational CDs, or lectures by
Deepak Chopra or the Dalai Lama. My suggestion was
not only ignored, but the music was switched to elevator versions of Clay Aiken's songs the next week.
Coincidence?

The only people I pity more than the staff are the customers. It's impossible to find anything here, and if you can
find it, you can't reach it. The stock boys are mostly too short
to reach up and help. In fact, the only tall person in the store
is Afrim, a six-foot-four beanpole from Kosovo who works
in the deli. He's very protective of his meats (especially the
Eastern European varieties), so unless you're the manager,
you'll never get Afrim out from behind the counter.

Eddie's is the worst for old people. Lots of them are frail
and use their shopping carts as walkers. I consider myself
the self-appointed helper of the aged. I make a point of

Allison van Diepen

knowing where the All-Bran is, the Ovaltine, the prunes and the denture cream.

One customer in particular got me onto the helping-old-people bandwagon. Her name is Lucy Ball—yes, it's true. She turned eighty-nine in August. She's less than five feet tall and doesn't mind that I call her Short Stuff. She's got a husband at home who had a stroke last year, so poor Lucy's in charge of keeping the house running. It isn't easy when you're hunched over like she is. I always help her by double-bagging everything, triple-bagging the meats, waiting patiently while she counts her pennies and just generally being nice to her. She told me I'm her favorite cashier, which doesn't say a lot considering the other cashiers here (well, except for Ryan), but it still makes me feel good. I know she means it because she'll go in my lineup even if it's the longest.

Yep, Lucy is a breath of fresh air in the hellish inferno of my workplace.

Half the customers here are escaped convicts or certified weirdos. Like the crazy cat lady who only buys three things: soda crackers, milk and cat food. And when I say cat food, I mean, like, seventy cans. She does this every week. I wonder how many cats (or cat ladies) it takes to eat all that.

And Mom wonders why I complain about this job.

Yeah, working at the Hellhole shows me how important it is to get an education. If I don't, I might have to work at a place like this my whole life. That's the best work-ethic lesson Mom could hope for.

"IT'S GOT SOME POTENTIAL," Jared says of my latest sketch. He's been trying to help me lately, or so it seems. I think he finds my attempts at drawing entertaining. Like right now, he's biting his lip to keep from laughing. "The head's too big for the body, though."

I shouldn't be putting up with him, but I'm keeping him around in the event he can actually help me. Also, he smells good.

"Why couldn't I just use that photo of the Afghan girl? This one is so…blah."

"I thought you wanted to start off playing 'Chopsticks' instead of Mozart."

"Okay, fine. How do I get the head the right size?"

"Why don't you just measure it?"

I do, and within a few minutes I produce a fairly ac-curate head. Now I have to sketch the tall supermodel body. Jared's right that the picture is simple, though I have an aversion to drawing unnaturally skinny women.

"So, how'd you end up at this school?" I ask. He's one of the few new kids this year.

His eyes narrow a fraction. At least I think they do. His face doesn't give much away. "This school had a space."

"Where were you before?"

"Sunset Park."

"I hear Sunset Park can be pretty rough."

"It's different."

I decide to pursue a different line of questioning. "You're a senior, right? I saw you were in grade twelve English."

"Are you stalking me, Kayla?"

I feel myself blush. "I'm just observant."

"Yeah, I'm a senior."

Well, that explains why he's old enough to shave. Suddenly I wonder if he has hair on his chest, or if he's like Case Study No. 2 who had, like, three hairs.

Realizing that I'm staring at his chest, I look up.

"Are you a fan?" he asks.

"Huh?"

"You're funny, you know that? I'm asking if you like them."

Oh, he means the band Three Days Grace. He's wearing a black T-shirt with the band's name and the words *Animal I Have Become.*

"I'm not a fan. Not really."

"What do you listen to? Miley Cyrus?"

Coming from him, I know that's an insult. "Yeah, definitely," I say with a straight face. "But the Jonas Brothers are even better."

Jared makes a gagging noise, and I laugh.

"Truth is, I mostly listen to Top 40 stuff, but not them. What about you?"

"Anything with a good tune and lyrics that mean something. You know, bands that actually write and play their own music. Not groups that recycle the same tunes over and over."

"Do you play anything?"

"Guitar. I'm in a band called The Invisible. A couple of guys at this school are in it, too—Tom Leeson and Said Abdullah."

"Tom sang at the coffeehouse last year. He was good."

"What about you, you play anything?"

"I played violin in junior high, but I guess that doesn't count. I'm not very musical."

"Maybe you haven't discovered it yet."

"Sure."

I can't help thinking—he's in a band. Bands mean popularity, groupies. So why don't I see him surrounded by people in the hallways and having lunch with the A-list crowd?

I'm starting to think that Jared isn't so much a snob as a loner, someone who stays deliberately outside the mainstream.

Maybe he can use the help of the Oracle...

AFTER THE SEVENTH-PERIOD bell, I make my move. When I'm sure the hallway is clear, I slip a business card into Jared's locker.

Need Dating Advice?
Contact the Oracle of Dating at 555-DATE.
Or visit the Oracle online at oracleofdating.com.

When my next class ends, I hurry to my locker in time to see Jared open his. The card flutters to the ground. He picks it up, makes a face and shows it to Andrew Becker.

Oh, no! He's asking Andrew if he got one, too!

Andrew shakes his head.

Jared tosses the business card on the floor.

Damn it!

So much for that idea. How am I supposed to help Jared now?

I grab my history book and close my locker.

It's a lesson everyone in the caring professions has to learn at some point. You can't force people to accept your help. They have to want it.

four

THE THIRD WEEK OF SEPTEMBER is when classes choose their Student Council reps. Believe it or not, I'm class rep for 11B.

How did I manage that? Amy nominated me and I didn't say no. And then one of the popular girls—Brooke Crossley's number one follower, Kirsten Cook—gets nominated. After that, no one else wants to run. So we leave the classroom while everybody votes. No secret ballot, just a show of hands in front of the teacher. Kirsten doesn't talk to me in the hallway but uses her cell phone to book a bikini wax. I wonder who she's dating and what she's doing to need a bikini wax.

We go back in. Mr. Findley says that I won. I say, "Really?"

And then Kirsten puts a hand on her hip and goes, "Are you sure?"

And I say, "Yeah, are you sure?"

Allison van Diepen

"I'm sure."

After class, Amy explains what happened. It was unbelievable! Sean Fortier said to Alfred Weams that the nerd crew better vote for Kirsten. And Alfred was like, *"Are you kidding me? Kirsten doesn't even say hi to us. Kayla is way cool."* Apparently it came down to the nerds versus the popular crowd, a power struggle as old as time. And the nerds' will prevailed because they outnumbered the popular crowd.

Which leads me to today's meeting. I'm sitting beside Ellen Huang, who has a romance novel perched behind her lunch bag so Prez Kevin Markinson doesn't see.

I'm not listening, either. I'm trying to read the book over her shoulder. It must be good, because Ellen hasn't looked up in the past ten minutes.

"Tears welled up in her blue eyes. She could have wept with the need to touch his face, to smooth the angry scowl from his brow. Oh, to feel his lips against hers one more time. But it was impossible…"

"That's some book," I whisper.

Ellen grins. "I've got the whole series at home if you want to borrow it."

"Series? Are they all four hundred pages?"

"Yeah, but you won't want them to end, trust me."

"Is there a lot of sex in them?"

"Hell, yeah. How do you think the author fills up four hundred pages? I'll bring you the first book tomorrow. You're going to get hooked."

It's about time I see what all the fuss is about. I've never read any romance novels, especially not this sexy historical stuff. There has to be something to them if they're so popular.

"Girls." Ms. Verdel, staff adviser to the Student Council, is giving us a look that says, *shut up.* I don't understand why someone who hates young people is a teacher, much less Student Council adviser.

I tune in to Kevin Markinson. "…hoping a few of you will volunteer to fundraise for the Cancer Society. Last year we had bake sales at lunch and at parent-teacher conferences. We also had a penny harvest and the class that raised the most money won a pizza party. We need volunteers to organize these things."

The room falls silent. No hands go up.

"C'mon, guys. This is for cancer research!" Kevin looks over at Brooke. "Please."

"I don't have time. I'm cheerleading, like, every day."

"Chris?"

"I did it last year. Why don't you ask Joe?"

"Sorry," Joe says before Kevin can even ask him. "I'm on the football team."

"What about *her?*" someone says. "She's new. She hasn't done anything yet."

I know without looking up that *her* is me.

There is no way I can wiggle my way out of this one. I can't exactly tell them the real reason I don't have any spare time.

"I'll organize something," I say.

"Great." Kevin looks relieved. "Maybe the bake sale?"

"I've got another idea."

"Like what?"

"Speed dating."

Everyone turns to look in my direction. I feel my face heat, as it always does when people stare at me. "It's…it's really popular these days. I'm sure we can get lots of people to pay ten bucks to be in it."

Ms. Verdel is frowning. "Let's see what the parents think of this."

Kevin shrugs. "I'm sure they'll sign permission forms. I think it's a great idea." He looks around. "Don't you think?"

People are nodding.

"You'd better put this before the principal," Ms. Verdel says.

"I will, no prob," Kevin replies. "Cool, we've got speed dating, then. This girl here—what's your name again? Kayla? Okay, Kayla's going to organize it. Now, we need someone to do the bake sale…"

I phase out.

So my speed dating night is going to be bigger than I originally thought. Why not? My powers of organization will be put to the test.

"Guys, I'm going to need your help," I tell my friends the next day in the caf. "It's for the Cancer Society."

"I baked cookies last year," Sharese says. "I don't mind doing it again."

"I'm not talking about the bake sale, but I'll still take you up on your offer to bake cookies. I'm going to organize a speed dating night."

"I thought you were doing that for your sociology assignment," Viv says.

"I am. This way it'll be for charity, too. I figure we'll try to have two games with ten guys and ten girls in each. We could charge ten bucks a person. If we fill all the spots we can rake in four hundred bucks."

"Where are you going to have it?" Ryan asks.

"I was thinking we'd do it here at school, maybe in the library. We'd need to have a teacher there to chaperone— shouldn't be hard to find one. We could have a session from seven to eight, and one from eight to nine."

"If we do it in the library, they'd better let us decorate," Ryan says. "That place doesn't exactly say romance."

"Does that mean you're volunteering to do it?"

"Of course I am."

"Yay! And we'll need lots of refreshments. I was thinking we could sell drinks and snacks. Sharese?"

"I'll make my s'more cookies. They're gooey and delish. And I'll make cupcakes and Oreo Rice Krispie squares, too." Sharese is definitely the domestic one among us. Ryan runs a close second, but his line is fashion and decor.

"I'll bring some Indian food," Viv adds.

"Perfect." I write all of this down. "The biggest job of all is recruiting. We need twenty guys and twenty girls to fill up the two games. We have to get their money in advance in case people back out at the last minute. Are you guys gonna play?"

Sharese and Viv nod.

Ryan shrugs. "Maybe I'll sell the snacks and drinks."

"Great, I could use your help. As for advertising, we can make posters and put them around the school. And I'll write something for the morning announcements."

"When are we doing this?" Sharese asks.

"I was thinking we could do it two weeks from Friday. Another thing—everyone will need to have a permission form signed by a parent."

They groan.

"I know, I know. We just need to cover our asses in case somebody gets upset and tries to sue the school."

"It's so stupid," Sharese says. "I'm old enough to drive but not to sit across from a guy for five minutes without mommy's permission!"

"Pretty much. Actually, Ms. Verdel warned us not to recruit anyone younger than sixteen."

"So we leave out half the school?" Ryan asks. "That's B.S."

"We just have to live with it. Amy's agreed to help out, too. She says she'll get Chad to bring some jocks on board. The girls will love that. We might even have to organize a few more games. Plus, I'm going to get Brooke and her friends there."

"You think Brooke will go for something this cheesy?" Sharese asks.

Ryan gives an exaggerated nod. "She totally will. That girl loves to be loved. There's nothing better for her ego than this."

"She *is* on the rebound from Declan," Viv points out. "This could be the perfect way for her to get out there again. Why don't you go ask her, Kayla? You won't find a better chance than this."

"Good point." I walk up to the table of cheerleaders and jocks, carefully measuring my steps so I don't go splat on the soda-slick floor in front of them. I tap Brooke on the shoulder. She turns around with a smile. See? She's really not as bitchy as everyone says.

"Can I talk to you for a second? Student Council stuff."

"Okay." She gets up, dusts the sandwich crumbs off her hands and steps back from the table.

"I know you're super busy with cheerleading, but I need your help in getting the speed dating off the ground. All you need to do is say you'll come and bring a few of your friends."

She crinkles her nose. "Why does it matter if we show up?"

Like she doesn't know. Time for a little ego-stroking—it *is* for a good cause.

"Guys are always drooling over you, Brooke. If they know you're going to be there, they'll be lining up for a ticket."

She smiles. "What kind of guys are going to be there?"

"Let's put it this way—Chad Douglas is recruiting from the soccer team. And, personally, I think a soccer bod is better than a football bod."

Her eyes glaze over as she thinks of the possibilities. "I'm in. I'll bring five girls with me. Maybe more."

"Perfect."

AROUND EIGHT O'CLOCK that night, an instant message pops up on my screen.

Loveless23: Oracle?

Oracle: Yes. I'm here.

Loveless23: I read your blog on flirting and I don't think I'm any good at it.

Oracle: Like anything else, you can improve with practice.

Loveless23: I don't even think I want to learn how to flirt. I just want the person I like to know that I like her. But I don't know how to do it.

Oracle: Are you too shy to be direct and ask her out?

Loveless23: Yeah. I can't see doing that.

Oracle: You could do it in a more subtle way. You could say you have two movie passes and your friend cancelled on you. And then see if she offers to join you.

Loveless23: That's not a bad idea. I doubt she'll want to go with me, though.

Oracle: Why do you say that? Are you picking up signals that she isn't interested?

Loveless23: I'm getting mixed signals. If she's interested, she doesn't know it yet. I don't think she sees me as a possible boyfriend.

Oracle: Why not? You must have some reason for saying that.

Loveless23: Well, she's really good-looking, for a start. She probably only goes out with GQ types. And she's a few years older than me.

Oracle: How much older?

Loveless23: My mom's age. No, I'm kidding. She's a couple years older than me, I think. And she has more seniority at work. I just don't think she really sees me. But I can't be too straight with her about how I feel—I know it would be a mistake.

Oracle: Why don't you just Be?

Loveless23: What does that mean?

Oracle: Show this girl who you are. Show her that you're funny and smart and compassionate (if you are those things). Then watch for signs that she's noticing you. If you don't get any, then it isn't meant to be. If you do, then find the courage to ask her to go for a drink after work.

Loveless23: What sort of signals am I looking for?

Oracle: She'll be looking at you more than she has to. And when you catch her, she'll either smile deeply into your eyes, or look away.

```
Loveless23: And if she doesn't look my way at all?
Oracle: Then somebody else will. Someone who will be apprecia-
tive of all you have to offer.
Loveless23: I got you, Oracle. Thanks.
Oracle: Good luck, Loveless23.
```

Nice. Another five bucks in the Oracle's shallow pocket.

It's refreshing to get a question from a guy for a change, especially one who's wondering if a girl is interested in him. Usually it's the other way around. Of the eight contacts I've had this week, half of them have been from girls wanting confirmation that a guy likes them. Those questions are always tricky, especially since my clients want one answer and one answer only. I ask them questions in order to assess the evidence: Does he go out of his way to talk to you? Do you chat with him online, and if so, who starts the conversation? Does he find ways to touch you when it's not necessary? The problem is, the girls themselves aren't a reliable source of information. They want the guy to like them, and so they present "evidence" to get me to confirm it, when really they're reading too much into what the guy has done.

All of this leaves me in a tight spot. If I tell these girls what they want to hear, they may be happy temporarily, but they might blame me if the guy turns out not to be interested. If I tell them that, based on the evidence, the odds are slim that the guy's into them, they'll probably never call me again. Most of the time, I have enough evidence to say the odds are fifty/fifty, and then I give them further strategies to discover the answer themselves.

I move from the computer to my bed, careful to keep my music low in case there's a *bling* signaling an instant message, or a *ping* signaling an e-mail.

I'm aware that your bedroom says a lot about you. Mine says a lot of different things. There are no major color schemes. The walls are white. I have some pictures up of me and my friends, and postcards from my sister's travels. The top of my dresser is devoted to jewelry and makeup, most of it lying out in the open instead of neatly arranged in the organizer I got last Christmas.

I have one stuffed animal on display. He's a brown scraggly mountain bear named Tanner. He's dressed in khakis as if he's an explorer on an expedition. He has a scowl on his face but a spark of humor in his eyes. Tanner is the only stuffed animal I haven't tucked away in a corner of my closet. He was a gift that my late grandfather brought back from Jamaica when I was seven. Ever since, Tanner has watched over me, more of a quiet companion than a toy.

I suppose Tanner reflects my sentimental side.

I have a romantic poster on my wall. It's black and white, showing a couple on a cobblestone street in Paris. The man is trying to sweep the woman off her feet, but he's only caught one leg so far. I like it because she still has one foot on the ground, like she's trying not to get swept away. She's giddy with romance, but one foot stays forever on the ground.

I bought my sister the same photo on a postcard, hoping she'd see it the same way and the message would stick.

My desk looks messy and disorganized, but I know where most things are. To the left of the monitor, I have a stack of books for when the Oracle needs some help. Callers like it when I quote a passage from, say, John Gray's classic *Men Are From Mars, Women Are From Venus*. I always say where the quotation is from, which impresses the callers even more, like they think I'm reciting it by memory instead of reading it. I have loads of pages book-marked and passages highlighted.

In order to explain having all these books, I told Mom and the Swede that I want to be a relationship counselor one day, which is true.

A few of the books are borrowed from Mom's office at the church. Part of being a minister is counseling families and couples. Some of the books in her office are for people who need help with their sex lives. When I asked her if she really loaned those books to couples, she said, "Oh, yes. Sexual problems are very common. Some-times they're so complicated I recommend that people see sex therapists." Mom winked at me. "Erland and I don't need that. We're very compatible."

I recoiled in horror. "Ugh, Mom! Too much information!"

I pick up the romance novel beside my bed. I'm halfway through it, though I only started it last night. From the moment the characters met, I couldn't put it down, just like Ellen promised. Even though she told me the book was full of sex, it's page 204, and they haven't done the deed yet. I know what she meant, though. From the first page, the story dripped with sexual tension. It's in the way the hero and heroine look at each other, the slightest touch, the innuendo in their words and the fiery passion of their kisses. It's this sexual tension that keeps me turning the pages, not the sex itself, which doesn't happen until page 286 (I flipped ahead, I admit it). It's all about the romance, the lust, the raw anticipation.

In my mind's eye I glimpse Jared Stewart poised over one of his sketches, his jaw tight, his eyes calculating as he decides what to draw next. Then he turns to me, his blue eyes darkening, his irises enlarging, his hard mouth turning up at the corner in a sexy smile. A feeling of heat comes over me, an inner melting, and I bite my lip.

Whatever! I mentally press Backspace, deleting the previous image. Okay, so I'm not immune to sexual tension. It's nothing to be ashamed of. I'm human.

Back to thinking like the Oracle. Tracey and her friends have always told me that the most exciting part of a relationship is the beginning—it's the newness, the anticipation, the early fireworks. It's the burning desire, not necessarily the fulfillment of that desire. In fact, that's one of the reasons Tracey agrees with me that she should wait a month before sleeping with a guy, no matter how crazy she is about him. It's because the longer they wait to fulfill their desire, the more intense those first weeks of dating are. In the end, though, most of her relationships, and those of her friends, don't last the first month.

All of this leads me to wonder: if women like sexual tension, often as part of a package called romance, what do guys want? And what do guys *my age* want? Most of them aren't reading romance novels, that's for sure.

Hmm… Maybe if I investigate what guys are reading, I'll have a better idea of what they're looking for in girls. This is something my female clients are always asking me. With a little P.I. work into the realm of *guy lit,* I hope I'll be able to tell them.

five

I'M NOTHING IF NOT DETERMINED.

"Can I see that?" I indicate the graphic novel Jared is reading, since he already finished his art assignment for the day.

He passes it to me. The first pictures I see make my eyes bug out: men in skin-tight suits with ridiculously extreme muscles; women with huge breasts and hips, dressed in silver galaxy-wear.

"This is what you guys are reading?"

"I don't know what you mean by *you guys,* but there are some good series out there."

"Are your friends reading this, too?"

"Most guys I know don't read anything but video game instructions."

"Seriously? Do the women in video games look like

this?" I open the book to a picture of a half-naked woman holding a machine gun.

"It's much worse in video games. Like in Grand Theft Auto, you can pick up a prostitute, then back over her with the car when you're done."

"Please tell me you're kidding."

"I'm not kidding. Why are you asking me this? Are you doing a project on what guys are reading?"

"I'm curious, that's all."

"Don't let the pictures fool you. Graphic novels usually have strong women in them. They just happen to be sexy, too."

"Sexy? You find this sexy?"

"It's fantasy, Kayla. Nothing to get all femme-Nazi about. This series actually has a good story line if you bother to read it."

"Looks like a *very* interesting story." I flip through the pages, seeing other sexual images.

"I don't think it's worse than those magazines you girls read. It's all about being gorgeous for guys, right? Clothes you can't afford and dumb dating advice like, *Ten Ways to Get a Guy*."

How the hell did he manage to hit a nerve like that? "There's nothing wrong with dating advice. It's meant to help people."

"C'mon, you know it's all a gimmick."

"Some of them, maybe. Not all of them."

I try to hand him back the book, but he says, "Hang on to it. Read it when you have the chance."

"Okay." I tuck it into my book bag. "Did you hear about the speed dating night we're organizing for the Cancer Society?"

"I heard the announcement." He looks suspicious now. "You want to recruit me."

"It's only ten bucks and it's for a good cause. You can bring as many friends as you want, just let me know ahead of time so we can reserve spots for them."

"You don't need to sell it. I'll go as a favor to you."

"Thanks. I'm sure it'll be fun."

"Yeah, right."

GUYS HAVE NO RIGHT to be this bizarre," Corinne complains. "They're all certifiably insane!"

Tracey and I nod in commiseration. It's Friday night at a crowded, overpriced sushi restaurant, and we're stuffed into a tiny corner table, which we waited an hour for. It's all part of dining in Manhattan, though, and I feel privileged to be invited out with Tracey and her BFF.

Corinne is an unnatural blonde who's been celebrating her twenty-fifth birthday for the past four years. She's an accountant who is bored with her job most of the year and sleeps in her office during tax season. Right now Corinne is using chopsticks to shove pieces of cold, wet fish into her mouth.

"So I'm at this guy's place and he cooks me this gorgeous shrimp paella—I didn't even tell him I was on the South Beach Diet. And then—get this—after dinner, we're sitting at the table lingering over our wine, and he starts flossing!"

Tracey and I look at each other in horror.

"It was on the kitchen counter behind him, as if that's its usual place. He didn't even have to leave the table to get it. He just—he just reached back!" Corinne is obviously still traumatized.

"Did you ask him to stop?" I ask.

"No. I should have. But the flossing didn't last very long. He's very efficient."

"Maybe it's a cultural thing," I say. "Where did you say he was from?"

"Queens."

"Oh."

"I heard Jerry Seinfeld flosses obsessively," Tracey says. "But he does have nice teeth."

"So are you going to see him again?" I ask. "The flossing thing doesn't have to be a deal-breaker."

"I know. I'll see him again—if he calls."

If he calls. That's what it's come to in Manhattan these days. Even after weeks of dating and nights of intimacy, the *if he calls* always hovers.

How many times has Tracey raved about a great date,

sometimes a great third or fourth date, only to never hear from the guy again?

No wonder most women in New York City suffer from dating paranoia.

"How'd it go with Scott yesterday?" Corinne asks Tracey.

"Scott?" I almost choke.

Tracey turns pink. "It was nothing. We just went for coffee after work."

I'm having trouble restraining all of the curses jumping onto my tongue.

"He says he misses our friendship."

"Friendship?" I pray for strength. Don't get emotional, Oracle. Tracey doesn't listen when you're emotional. She's a computer geek, she only listens to logic. "That's a classic way of reeling you back in, Trace. You're too smart to fall for it, right?"

"I sure am. He was pathetic, really. Starts telling me how lonely he's been these past few months, and I'm thinking, who cares?"

Ah, but she does care. I know she does. I stab a California roll with a chopstick. "What happens next time he asks you?"

She shrugs one shoulder like it's a no-brainer. "I say I'm busy."

"That's not enough, Trace. You say *no.* If you say you're busy, he'll just ask you another time. Trust me, say *no.*"

Allison van Diepen

Corinne nods. "Even if he just wants to be friends, that guy was a jackass. He doesn't deserve your friendship."

"Cheers to that." Corinne and I knock chopsticks.

"You're right, you're both totally right." But I can see the wheels in Tracey's head turning.

I don't get it. Why are many people drawn to someone who's hurt them? Maybe it's an ego thing—being hurt sucks, and you think you can erase that hurt by going back to the person who caused it. Then it will be like it never happened in the first place. Only problem is that it *did* happen.

Corinne is looking at me. "Any cute guys on the horizon?"

"Not really."

"But you're the Oracle of Dating—the expert! And you're so adorable! All the guys must be after you."

Reminding myself that I have an image to protect, I say, "I'm too busy for a boyfriend, but a fling or two might be in order."

"Now, that's the spirit—play the field!" She turns to Tracey. "Your sister's awesome. Why can't *we* be that way—all about having fun? Maybe we should aim for flings instead of relationships. We always end up getting burned, anyway."

"But in the long term, would you really be happy going from one man to another?" Tracey asks her. "There's a reason we're wired to want stable relationships. I think you should hold out for what you want."

"Good point." Corinne raises her glass. "Here's to holding out for the happy ending we deserve!"

We clink glasses.

"And if he can't be found in Manhattan, there's always Alaska," I add.

THE WEEK LEADING UP to my birthday flies by, and this is one of those lucky years when my birthday falls on a Saturday. I know I'm home free by Friday, the day of the art field trip. It won't be a glamorous ride into Manhattan, since Gerstad rented a yellow school bus, but it could be worse: I could be in class.

I dare a bathroom run before the bus door opens, and end up being the last person to board. I head to the back, the very back, and find that Lauren, the person I know best in this class, is sitting beside her friend Cara. So I make a split-second decision to sit beside Jared. I hope he doesn't mind. I'm sure he loves being the cool loner at the back, but I had few options, and he was the best-smelling one.

The bus starts with a jerk and whips around a corner. I have to clutch the seat in front of me so that I don't slide into Jared's lap. He takes out one of his earbuds. "Better get comfortable. It's gonna be forty-five minutes at least."

"I'll try, but if he makes a few more turns like that, it'll be cozier than you bargained for."

"Oh, yeah?" I catch a flash of heat in his eyes.

Oh. My. God. Without even meaning to, I just dove

into some heavy flirtation. And he sure as hell flirted back. There's wickedness in his blue eyes, and I can't help but wonder if he's done *it* before. And if he has, if he's good at it. And if he is, does he approach it the way he does his sketches, always looking for better techniques.

His eyes rake over me, and my mouth is bone-dry. "Don't you have an MP3?" he asks.

"I usually don't bring it to school."

"Too much talking with friends. No time for music."

"What are you listening to?"

"Vengeance Against the Establishment."

I laugh. It comes out as a girlish giggle, unfortunately.

"What's so funny?"

"It's a classic name. I bet a band with a name like that has mass appeal, even if their gimmick is that they don't care about the music industry. I'm not saying their music isn't good."

"It is good. But I see what you mean. These guys are pretend anarchists. They say they don't give a shit who they appeal to, and then they get all glammed up for *Rolling Stone*."

"Yeah, they speak out against the commercialization of music, but they're not exactly shying away from the spot-light."

He stares at me for a few seconds. "I'm starting to think you're as cynical as I am. That's cool."

"So which are you? A pretend anarchist or a real one?"

"I'm not an anything. I don't buy into any belief system. These days my foster mom, Gina, is always begging me to go to mass with her. She just wants to confess her sins and get out of there. Tries to get me to confess, but I won't. *She's* the one who runs an illegal business, not me."

"Are you serious? What does she do?"

"She sells lingerie and kinky stuff to transvestites. If you look at the back of the *New York Post,* she's always advertising her products."

"You're kidding me. And she's your *foster mom?*"

"Best one I ever had. Maybe taking me in is a way to atone for her sins, like the fact that she doesn't have a business license and she's not paying taxes. I think she's lived a wild life. Gina's, like, seventy-five—she won't tell me exactly how old. But she's not like the other foster parents I've had—she doesn't do it for the money. She doesn't treat me like a piece of furniture. She's a good person. A businesswoman through and through. If you know a guy who needs sexy lingerie, I'll put him in touch with her." Jared doesn't seem embarrassed about any of this. I bet he has a thousand crazy stories.

"You must have some weird people coming in and out of the house."

"I rarely run into anyone. When I do, they look down like they're embarrassed. These guys are shy and pretty normal-looking. They don't want anyone to know."

"So how long have you been at Gina's?"

"About two years."

"Where were you before that?"

"Got bounced from one home to another since I was ten. My mom's messed up on drugs. Never knew my dad." He shrugs. "I'll be eighteen at the end of June. Free to go my own way for a change."

I'm shocked that he's being so open. I don't know what to say except, "I'm sorry."

"For what?"

"It must've been rough."

"Don't do that."

"Do what?"

"The pity thing."

"Oh. Sorry."

"There it is again. Relax, Kayla. We've all dealt with our own shit, haven't we?"

True, but I doubt my parents' divorce and the arrival of the Swede match what he's been through.

"Rodrigo, my social worker, says we're on this earth for a reason. And some of us are dealt a shittier hand than others, but if we can overcome it, we can do big things. I know it sounds cheesy. He explains it better than I do." As if he's suddenly embarrassed, he glances out the window. "When I was in juvie, I made a decision to turn around for myself, not for anyone else. I'm sick of being part of the system—the foster care system, the detention system. So I keep my head down and live my life. Know what I mean?"

"Yeah. Definitely." Definitely not. He's been in *juvie?* I probably shouldn't ask why. It's none of my business.

"I stole things." He turns back to me, crooking his mouth. "What, you think I'd beat up an old lady or something?"

"You better not have. I like old people."

He's studying my face, as if he's gauging how I'm responding to all this. He probably thinks I'm sheltered. I guess I am.

But it's weird. I like that he's looking at my face. That we're close together in the cocoon of the bus seat. It's like we're in our own little world. And he's so cute it makes my stomach queasy. Now that I know his background, there's something even more raw, something *dangerous,* about him.

I shouldn't be more attracted. But I am.

A sheltered girl being attracted to a dangerous guy. Talk about cliché. The Oracle side of me would have a field day.

There's another presence here between us, a presence I didn't entirely recognize until now. A presence that rears up when a guy and a girl get close, when there's only two inches of bus seat between them, and their thighs are almost touching.

Sexual tension.

It's just like in the romance novel I'm reading. My heart is fluttering and my bosom (meager as it is) is heaving.

I glance at him. His eyes twinkle, as if he's amused. He must feel it, too.

Dear Crazed and Confused,

Don't worry—your problem is not unique. In fact, many people are attracted to their classmates. The Oracle herself has experienced sexual tension—

I delete my response. Okay, I'll admit it. A certain school bus episode is preventing me from concentrating. It's ridiculous, really. It's not like we spent the afternoon strolling around the museum together. Jared went off by himself, and I hung out with Lauren and Cara. On the way back, he was the last one on the bus. I'd sort of tried to save a seat for him, but eventually someone asked to sit there, and I couldn't say no. If he'd wanted to sit with me, wouldn't he have made an effort to get on the bus sooner?

I remind myself that I'm not in the market for a boyfriend. And even if I were, it would be ridiculous to bet on a guy who's been in juvie. While I'm comforted that he wasn't locked up for a violent crime, stealing is still very serious. I doubt they put you in juvie for stealing candy bars or CDs. It's probably something bigger, like a car. Or what if he stole a kid's bicycle—how cruel is that?

True, Jared says that he's turned around. It doesn't sound like it was a moral epiphany so much as the fact that he didn't want to be part of the juvie system anymore. Fair enough. But Dr. Phil does say that the best predictor of future behavior is past behavior.

Okay, so I'm sounding judgmental. I'm not saying that

if I dated him I'd have to lock up my purse in a safe or anything. It's just well-known that when couples have similar backgrounds, their relationship has a higher chance of success. Our backgrounds couldn't be more different. And while the idea that opposites attract is true, opposites don't generally stay together.

This is the universe conspiring to tempt me, that's what it is. And I don't know why I'm wasting time thinking about this, because a perceived moment of sexual tension doesn't mean he's interested in me at all. He's probably used to girls being intrigued by his bad-boy past and drooling over his gorgeousness. I bet he finds the whole thing as funny as my ridiculous drawings in art class.

six

It's hard to believe I'm turning sixteen. I feel old.

Ms. Goff always tells us it's a myth that high school is the best time of your life. She says we should count ourselves lucky if we get through it with only a few emotional scars. She says the older we get, the more freedom we'll have to study what we want, work at a job we want and hang out with the people we want. Amy thinks she's just saying that to make the depressed people in the class feel better.

But I kind of agree with Ms. Goff. Being a teen isn't easy with so many reeling emotions, whirling hormones, excruciating classes and heinous part-time jobs. According to Oprah, our twenties are pretty much a write-off, too. She says that in your twenties, you're confused, struggling to find your place in the world and chasing after the wrong kind of men.

Fast-forward to when I'm thirty. Maybe then, I'll have a great career, great guy and great hair.

And now they're saying forty is the new thirty. And fifty is the new forty. And sex after fifty is better than ever because you're suddenly unselfconscious and free, even though your body isn't what it was when you were twenty. I don't want to wait until I'm fifty to be comfortable with myself and have good sex!

Maybe that's why Mom's friend, Sister Margaret, left the convent at age fifty-two to marry Father Caldwell. She was waiting for the good sex!

If I keep thinking like this, my head will explode.

DAD NEVER FORGETS my birthday. It's programmed into his BlackBerry and reminders pop up every hour until he calls me.

"Happy sweet sixteen, Mickey!"

I cringe. He's been calling me that since I was a baby. I told him I hated it the moment I was able to speak. I am not Mickey Mouse.

"What are you doing tonight, Mickey? Going out for dinner?"

"Mom, Erland and Tracey took me out for lunch. Tonight I'm going out with my friends. I don't know where. It's a surprise."

"That's great! You know, you should fly up for the weekend one of these days. It's only an hour flight."

Dad invites me to Ottawa all the time. One of these days I'll have to go. But playing tourist with my dad isn't my idea of a fun time, especially when I'll have to make nice with his girlfriend of the month. I don't know how he gets women, all at least a decade younger than he is. He hasn't aged half as well as Mom.

The conversation drones on for another twenty minutes until his cell goes off. "I've got to take this."

"What's her name?"

He laughs. "Her name is Megan. I hope you'll meet her when you come to visit. Bye for now, honey. I love you."

"Love you, too, Dad." Somehow it never feels honest when I say it. It's not that I don't love him. I do.

I just don't like him much.

BIRTHDAYS ARE A BIG DEAL to my friends. They're an excuse to shop for gifts, eat too much and find ways to drink. For Amy's birthday we got our hands on some rum and had a bush party. One bottle of rum doesn't go a long way among five people, though. I didn't even get a buzz.

Viv turned sixteen in August. Her party was hosted by her parents and attended by a hundred relatives and family friends. I ate too many samosas, had wicked gas and left early.

My friends are convinced that we should crank it up for my birthday. They tell me to pack for a sleepover and be at Ryan's at six sharp. When I arrive, everybody is already there, looking fabulous. I'm wearing my gift from Tracey, a candy-striped cami, with black skinny jeans and black suede booties. I hardly have the chance to sit down before my friends pelt me with gifts: a pair of earrings, a scarf, a chick-lit book, a personal manicure kit, a sampler of Victoria's Secret perfumes.

Ryan's parents are obviously away for the night, because he opens the liquor cabinet and uses his mom's smoothie maker to concoct piña coladas and strawberry daiquiris.

"Tonight is going to be wild," Ryan informs me.

"All your master plan, right?"

"Uh-huh. Drink up."

He doesn't have to convince me. I get a buzz going after the first drink. Yes, I'm a cheap drunk. Then I switch to water because I don't want to pass out on his couch at seven. That would not be conducive to having a good time.

We laugh and gossip and sing along to music. We do one another's hair and makeup. We take silly pics to post online.

Around ten, Ryan announces that we're heading out.

"Where are we going?" I ask as we pile into a cab.

"As if we're going to tell you!" Sharese fluffs my hair.

We go over the Manhattan Bridge and end up in a shady-looking part of the Meatpacking District.

"You can let us out here," Ryan says to the cab driver.

They're fumbling for cash to pay the driver. I go into my handbag and Sharese slaps my hand away. "Don't even think about it."

We follow Ryan around the corner. The neighborhood is looking no less shady. We lock arms. Ryan is walking farther and farther ahead of us.

After a couple of blocks, he runs back. "We're here. Ready with your IDs?"

I see them pull laminated cards from their handbags. Holy crap—they've got fake IDs!

Amy hands me mine.

"How'd you get these?"

"Chad has a contact."

I study the ID. Whoever Chad's contact is, he obviously has access to the Hunter College student ID template. Do you really think the bouncers are going to let us in with these?"

"If we don't blow it, they will," Ryan says. "They don't care if you're underage as long as you have some ID. Now, let's go."

My stomach does a little flip as we walk toward the entrance. There's a big door with the number 257 on it. Ryan knocks and the door opens.

A huge bald guy with a goatee looks us over. I'm so nervous I feel my knees knock together. His eyes stop on me. *Damn it! My baby face is going to blow it for us!*

But his gaze moves on. "ID?"

One by one, my friends give him their ID, he looks at it and lets them go in. I'm last and having heart palpitations.

He takes my ID and asks me, "When's your birthday?"

"Uh—today!"

"Happy twenty-first."

"Thanks!" I rush past him and join my friends. They're all paying the ten-dollar cover charge. I reach for my money and this time it's Viv who slaps my hand.

We walk down a flight of stairs. I can feel the heavy pump of music beneath us. At the bottom of the stairs, we go through a steel door. "Holy mother of—"

It's a massive underground storeroom transformed into a pimped-out club. Bloodred lights cast an eerie glow. The music is deafening. I don't recognize the song, it's just a solid hard beat. The dance floor is packed. There isn't much in the way of seating, only a few chairs, but then, this isn't a place for sitting.

Ryan snaps his fingers in front of my face. I must've been looking around like an idiot. "Drink?"

I nod, then hug him tight because I'm so happy to be here.

I can't believe it's my sixteenth birthday and I'm in a real club! This isn't one of those alcohol-free teen dance nights we sometimes go to. This is the real deal. Most people look like they're actually legal.

And there are a lot of cute guys around. At least, I think there are. It's hard to tell with the lights flashing.

My friends pull me onto the dance floor and we all lose our minds. The music is fast and frenzied. The beat pours through our blood and makes us dance with the spineless funk of jellyfish.

Ryan puts a drink in my hand and I guzzle it as I dance. I have a buzz from the music and the booze. There's a guy on the dance floor who keeps bumping into me. Can't he watch where he's dancing? Wait a minute—now he's grinding behind me. And he's actually pretty cute. I turn and we're dancing together. I wrap my arms around his shoulders, catching the scent of his cologne. He smells good. Not as good as Jared Stewart, but good. *Stop thinking about Jared!*

He's nuzzling my neck, sucking on it. I hope he doesn't give me a hickey. Ouch! I pull away. He apologizes and goes back to nuzzling.

I look over to see Sharese grinding with my guy's friend, and Amy grinding with some other guy.

Viv and Ryan are dancing together, but no grinding is involved.

I feel his lips move up to my mouth. I tilt my head toward him. His lips are on mine. It's been ages since I've kissed someone, and it feels damned good. I wonder what it would be like to kiss Jared. *Damn it, I've got to stop thinking about him!*

When the song is over, he takes my hand and buys me a drink at the bar. I don't take my eyes off the drink—I may be tipsy, but I've heard lots of stories of girls having date rape drugs slipped into their drinks.

The guy is talking to me but I can barely hear him. His name is Kevin or Devin or something. He's twenty-one and works as a bike courier. I can picture him weaving in and out of Manhattan traffic, fearless, his twelve-speed burning up the pavement, his hair flying in the wind (well, really, if he doesn't wear a helmet he's insane). I tell him I'm in high school. He's surprised, or at least pretends to be. He doesn't ask my age. I don't offer it.

I'm under no illusions about dating this guy. He's cute, but there's no real connection. Since the conversation doesn't go anywhere, we go back to the dance floor. By now Sharese and Amy are making out with guys. Amy's cheating on Chad! Wait—this isn't new; Amy's been known to make out with other guys behind Chad's back. And Ryan and Viv still have absolutely no interest in touching each other.

What's-his-name can hardly keep up with me, but he seems to enjoy trying. I do get a bit insane when I'm dancing. I think I was born to dance. Maybe I'll get spotted and asked to dance in a music video.

I know that time is going by, but as long as there's music, I'll be dancing. I hear the DJ announce last call. *Oh, no! I don't want this night to end!*

I'm still dancing with What's-his-name when the music goes off and the lights go on. He's got a few acne scars, but I don't hold that against him. Sharese and Amy say goodbye to their respective hotties, and I give Kevin (Devin?) one last kiss. We go to the bar, where he scrawls something on a napkin and gives it to me.

"Call me if you want." And with another dazzling kiss, we part.

Allison van Diepen

Sigh.

On the cab ride home, I uncrumple the napkin. It says: *Melvin 555-3456.*

"What is it? What'd he write?" Amy asks.

"His name is Melvin."

My friends crack up.

Sharese is ROTFLOL. "Melvin? Doesn't he have the decency to call himself Mel?"

"I guess not."

My friends are still laughing when my head rolls back against the seat and I conk out.

IF THERE WERE A CONTEST to name the most pathetic kid in school, Evgeney Vraslov would win hands-down. He is too nerdy even for the nerds to be seen with. He came from Bulgaria two years ago and still wears bell-bottoms and butterfly collars, as if his wardrobe comes from a seventies time capsule.

Evgeney's IQ is off the charts, but you wouldn't know by talking to him, since his accent is so strong that you can't tell if he's speaking English or Bulgarian. Even the Russian kids can't understand him. It doesn't help that Bulgaria is the only Eastern European country where the people shake their heads to say yes, and nod to say no.

"Evgeney wants to go speed dating? And you said *yes?*"

It's after school on Monday and I'm sitting at McDonald's with Amy.

"He has just as much right to go as anyone else," I say, a little defensively. "He's a nice guy."

"I'm not saying he isn't, but what happens when nobody checks him off? Don't you think he'll be devastated?"

I know what she's saying, which is why we're trying to recruit lots of different social groups to increase the chances of people liking each other. It's Amy's job to classify them, then slot them into the games.

As for Evgeney, it's unlikely that anyone will pick him. The fact that he probably knows this and is still willing to try makes me feel even worse for him.

"Let me see the list." Amy grabs my notepad and looks at it.

Paid Players as of September 26

<u>Guys</u>	<u>Girls</u>
Chris Ramos (J)	*Motria Chabon (A)*
Robbie Price (J)	*Brooke Crossley (C)*
Ben Mueller (N)	*Lauren Ellis (C)*
Victor Chan (N)	*Magda Goryeva (C)*
Shamar Edgars (J)	*Alena Ventris (J)*
Steven Williams (N)	*Vivian Gupta (N)*

Allison van Diepen

Jared Stewart (A)
Evgeney Vraslov (N)

Sharese Malcolm (A)

$$A = Artsy \quad C = Cheerleader$$
$$J = Jock \quad N = Nerd$$

"So we need twelve more guys and fourteen more girls to fill up the two games. That'll be easy. Lots of people still want to sign up, they just haven't paid yet. I still think we'll have enough for three games."

I hope she's right.

TIME: 5:03 P.M. One hour until showtime.

Amy's prediction proves right: we have three—count 'em, *three* speed dating lineups! In fact, so many people signed up in the past few days that we'll have twelve dates in each game.

As of now, all logistics are in place. Each game will take one hour, with a ten-minute intermission after the first six dates. There will be fifteen minutes in between games, hopefully enough time to get one group out and the next group seated. Tomorrow we'll compile the results. I've promised to send everyone an e-mail with their matches by five.

Thanks to Ryan, the library has been transformed. Most of the lights are off, except for the ones illuminating the back bookshelves. The custodial staff wouldn't allow candles, so Ryan brought three lamps from home and screwed in red light bulbs, creating a night-clubish ambience. He set up six dating tables, which he covered with white tablecloths and rose petals. The budget for decorating was twenty dollars, but Ryan insisted on making this his contribution to the evening.

I go over to the food table where Viv, Sharese and Amy are putting out snacks and drinks. Everything looks so good that my stomach reminds me it's dinnertime.

Allison van Diepen

Sharese says, "Go ahead, we have lots."

I don't argue and put some food on my plate. The girls laugh when, feeling guilty, I throw a few dollars into the box before scarfing down the food.

People start to arrive around quarter to six. I greet everybody and give them a game card on which they'll fill in their dates' names, circle yes or no, and write comments to remember them by later.

At six, we're missing five people for the first round. In the meantime, I tell the participants to take their seats at their assigned table.

By six-ten, we're still missing three people. We have an uneven number, eleven guys and ten girls. Amy volunteers to even it up.

Sharese, who's never shy to speak in public, stands up. "Welcome to speed dating! You should all have your cards in front of you. First thing, write your name at the top. The girls will stay in their seats and the guys will move to the table on their right every five minutes—we'll ring a bell to let you know. When five minutes are up, check off yes or no. Don't do it in front of them, please. Do it as you're moving to the next table or at the end of the game. We'll have a ten-minute break halfway through the game where you can get more refreshments. Happy dating!"

I stand behind the refreshment table with Ryan. He's arranging the napkins artfully, and like me, he's watching the daters. "Check out the hot vibe at table two."

I nod. "Table seven looks uncomfortable. And that guy at table six is teasing them. Are they exes, do you think?"

"They're brother and sister."

"Please tell me you're kidding."

"I'm not kidding. She's a senior and he's a junior. I guess since their last name is Smith, Amy didn't put it together."

"Crap. We could've easily put them in different games if we'd known. I hope they don't ask for their money back."

"They still have eleven *non*-blood-related dates. Isn't that enough?"

When my stopwatch beeps, I ring the bell. "Next date, everybody!"

And I ring the bell every five minutes until intermission, then we continue until the game is over. Afterward, several of the daters linger to fill in their cards, while others keep chatting with their dates. I suppose it's a good thing, but there's a bottleneck near the doors with people leaving and new daters coming in.

I signed up several of the people in the next game myself, like Jared, Brooke and Evgeney. I greet everybody as they come in, giving them their cards and pointing to their assigned seats. Some girls from the last game are still hanging around the library doors, complaining loudly about how the guys in this game are so much cuter than in the first game and how unfair it is.

One of them, Candace Granada, comes up to me with her hands on her hips. "Why did we get the lame-ass guys, huh? I heard there were going to be soccer players. Our group looked more like the chess team to me."

"We did the best we could placing people," I say apologetically.

"I told my girls we were gonna get dates out of this—what do I tell them now?"

Amy comes up, a sweet smile on her face. "Tell them the Cancer Society is very grateful for their support. Now, you'd better move along…"

To my relief, Amy takes control of the situation, ushering the girls out. Five minutes later, Sharese gives her spiel and starts the game.

I go back to the refreshment table, where Ryan is counting the money and the girls are replacing the snacks and drinks. "Twenty-three bucks for food and bev in the first game. Not bad."

"That's because of Sharese's Oreo Rice Krispie squares," Viv says.

Sharese shakes her head. "It's the pakoras."

"Actually, it was mainly the drinks," Amy says. Then, quietly, "Don't look now, but Brooke is sitting with Evgeney, and they're not even talking."

I do look, seeing Brooke filing her nails right in front of him. Couldn't she talk to the guy for five minutes? My heart squeezes with sympathy. Poor Evgeney.

The dates continue, one after another, with an intermission halfway. I'm sort of watching Jared out of the corner of my eye. I'm curious as to how he's getting along with the girls. There seems to be a lot of smiling and laughing. Well, on top of his cuteness, I guess he has a certain charm.

On the eighth date, the girl in front of him is Brooke. He keeps glancing down at her chest. That dog, I hope he doesn't make any matches—not even one!

But the weird thing is, besides the glimpses at her chest, he is talking to her and she is giggling and flipping her hair. You don't have to be the Oracle of Dating to see that she's enjoying herself.

Okay, so I realize that I am now in a bad mood and the obvious reason is not one I want to accept. Maybe

I'm annoyed that Brooke is flirting with Jared when she has no real intentions of dating him. Yes, that's it. I feel sorry that his little ego boost will be short-lived.

Damn it, why did Amy have to put him in the same round as Brooke?

When their time is up, I ring the bell with new enthusiasm.

The game ends, and I can see that the third-round daters are eagerly waiting at the library doors. As we let the second group out and the third in, Jared materializes at my elbow.

"Nice job with this."

God, his eyes are so blue. "Thanks," I say, handing out game cards as people stream past me in both directions.

He leaves, and I'm suddenly desperate to see who he checked off and who he didn't, but of course I have a job to do.

We get everyone seated and start the game with the first ring of the bell. I pick up the cards from the last game and count them to make sure they're all there. When I find Jared's card, I somehow feel guilty for looking at it, but then I remind myself that it's my job to look at all of the cards and compile the results.

His card looks like this:

1.	Angie	*no*	*easy on the perfume!*
2.	Sarah	*no*	*boring as hell*
3.	Erica	*no*	*lacking upstairs*
4.	Alena	*no*	*bites her nails big-time*
5.	Linden	*no*	*doesn't get me*
6.	Magda	*no*	*don't get her*
7.	Brooke	*no*	*tits are real, the rest is fake*

He said no to Brooke. Yay!!!

8.	Christie	*no*	*know-it-all*
9.	Anna	*no*	*doesn't know enough*
10.	Rena	*no*	*addicted to reality TV*
11.	Nickeema	*no*	*still depressed about Michael Jackson*
12.	Stephanie	*no*	*just not for me*

He said no to every girl. Wow. And then, this:

13. ___?___   *YES*   *she knows who she is*

What does that mean? Who is she?

seven

OF COURSE IT ISN'T ME, I tell myself when I'm back in my bedroom a couple of hours later. Whoever he's talking about would obviously know it.

Or maybe I'm taking his words too literally. Does "she knows who she is" mean that she is someone who is confident and knows what she's about? Maybe he doesn't mean one girl in particular. He could be making a general statement.

What do I do now? Call him and ask what this is all about?

Of course I'm not going to do that. Then he would totally think I like him. And I don't even know if I like him, or if I'm just attracted to him. Crazy, hotly attracted to him. I mean, I obviously like him a bit, but I'd have to know him better before I could gauge if we could have a real, meaningful relationship.

All I know is, a little bit of attraction—okay, *a lot* of

attraction—isn't cause to break my no-dating-until-college rule. Letting raging teenage hormones rule my brain will surely lead to heartbreak. I've seen it happen to countless friends and clients.

It's not fair. Biologically, I have no choice but to be attracted to him. Thinking back to all of the girls sitting across from him at speed dating, I realize they probably felt the same way. Jared is dark, brooding, strong and has a troubled past—he just screams romance-novel hero. How can anyone not be drawn to that?

And masculine. God, he just radiates masculine strength. Those arms. Those big hands. Not to mention the facial hair. And those smoldering dark blue eyes…

It's official: I'm a twisted fiend.

And it's all Jared's fault.

THE SMELL OF THE SWEDE'S pancakes, hours old by now, conspire with my grumbling tummy to get me out of bed around ten. I throw on a robe and slippers and trudge downstairs.

"Good morning, Kayla." The Swede has a cup of coffee and a magazine in front of him. "Pancakes are on the stove. You might want to reheat them in the microwave."

"Thanks." I put two of the thick circular pancakes on a plate, touch them and decide they're warm enough for me. "Can I have a cup of your coffee?"

He raises a brow. "Yes, but since when do you drink coffee?"

"I didn't sleep that well." I pour myself a cup, stir in some cream, then sit down and pour syrup onto my pancakes.

"What kept you awake?"

"I've been thinking about all the speed dating stuff." Which isn't completely untrue. I'm just not being specific about what part of the speed dating I was thinking about. The last thing I'm going to tell the Swede is that I'm thinking about a guy.

"How did it go?"

"Good. My friends are coming over this afternoon to put together the results."

"Did you make a match last night?"

"Erland."

"What did I say?"

"I wasn't trying to find a date. I didn't even participate. I had to run the thing."

"Oh, that is unfortunate."

"Why? You think I need a boyfriend?"

"Not necessarily a boyfriend, but perhaps a few dates."

"People my age don't go on a *few dates.* You pretty much have a boyfriend or you don't."

"That is a shame. I used to date many different girls when I was your age. We would go to the cinema or to a dance. Sometimes we would go driving. I do enjoy a drive on a nice day. Don't you?"

I can't believe this. The Swede, whom I've always thought of as a total square, probably had more fun as a teenager than I'm having.

"LOOK AT THIS!" Amy waves the dating card in her hand. The five of us are crammed into my bedroom. "Brooke said yes to Jared Stewart!"

I snatch the card from her hand. It's true. In the comments section, she even drew a heart.

"Let's see if he checked her off," Amy says.

Sharese finds his card. "He didn't. He didn't check anyone off. And at the end, he put a number thirteen and wrote, *she knows who she is*. Weird." She passes the card around.

"Maybe he means Kayla," Viv says. "He must've meant for one of us to see it. And don't you guys sit together in art class?"

"Yeah, but…I think he's just making a statement." But I have to wonder if Viv is right; why would he write that if he didn't intend for one of us to see it?

"I told you that kid was strange," Amy says. "He's the only guy who didn't check Brooke off. Maybe he's gay."

Viv scoffs. "You're saying any guy who doesn't like Brooke is gay? That's stupid."

"He liked her tits," Sharese says in Jared's defense.

Amy looks at his card. "'Tits are real, the rest is fake.' Is he implying that she got a nose job? I've always wondered about that."

"I think he's referring to her personality," I say. "Obviously he cares about more than her chest. He could be mature enough to know that boob size isn't everything."

"Well, *I* have a theory on why she checked him off. I bet dating some stoner would be her way of getting back at Declan."

"You think he's a stoner?" I'm trying to sound casual.

"Of course he is," Amy says. "He dresses like one. Anyway, no normal guy would pass up the chance for a boob-grope."

"Let's hurry up, guys." Sharese claps her hands. "I want to know who checked me off!"

"We're not telling you your results in person," I say. "You'll get them through e-mail."

"You're just saying that because nobody checked me off," Sharese says with mock sadness. "Well, I didn't check any of the guys off, anyway, because I only have eyes for Mike P."

"Fine, then. Darren Prince and John Culver checked you off."

"Oh, cool! What about Viv?"

Viv shakes her head. "I don't want to know now. Maybe later."

Sharese frowns. "C'mon, Viv. I bet Raj picked you!"

"Later, okay?"

"Her choice, guys." I look at Amy. "You didn't check anyone off, either."

"How could I? I'm already with Chad."

"That didn't stop you from making out with that guy on my birthday."

"At least his name wasn't Melvin! I still want to know how many guys checked me off."

Ryan rolls his eyes. "Somebody wants her ego stroked." He finds her results. "Eight of the guys checked you off, Amy. Are you happy now?"

"Yes. I'm happy now. I can't wait to tell Chad. He'll be so jealous."

Ignoring that, Viv asks, "Has anyone figured out how much money we made?"

"Yep." I have the number in front of me. "How about seven hundred and fifty-three dollars?"

We cheer and pound palms.

"My mom's ordering us pizza later," I tell them. "First we have to e-mail everybody with their results. That'll take a while. We'll save time if we use two computers. Sharese and Ryan can use the one in my mom's office."

Sharese yanks Ryan to his feet. I give them the information they need and they head down the hall.

Viv, Amy and I hit the computer. I realize as I'm turning my monitor on that oracleofdating.com is on the screen. Just as it's starting to light up, I click a button to reboot the computer. I'll have to be more careful the next time I have friends in my room.

We get to work, typing in e-mail addresses and sending short prewritten messages.

Congratulations, you have two matches! Their e-mail addresses are...

Or,

Sorry, you had no matches in this game. We'd like to thank you for supporting the Cancer Society.

"I told you Evgeney wouldn't get any matches," Amy says.

"I know. But he deserved a chance like everyone else." I feel bad for him, though.

Amy's cell rings, and she decides to take it outside. I ask Viv if we can talk about her results. She nods.

"You didn't pick anyone, Viv. I had two Indian guys there and both checked you off. You didn't want to give either of them a chance?"

"Not really."

"What about Max McIver?"

"Did he check me off?"

"You're the only one he checked off."

Her face is unreadable. "Oh."

"Do you want to change your mind and check him off now?"

"No. We'd better get this done, Kayla. I'm starting to get hungry for the pizza."

We go back to work. But the Oracle is convinced there's more weighing on Viv's mind than pizza.

Allison van Diepen

What Gives? An Examination of the New Trend in Modern Romance Called Speed Dating

By Michaela Cruickshank

My project was to conduct a speed dating experiment as a fundraiser for the Cancer Society.

The speed dating phenomenon is based on the premise that people can tell within a short period of time whether they have any romantic interest in someone. In my experiment, a male and female student would sit across from each other for five minutes with the aim of assessing whether they would like to date that person. After the five-minute bell, the boys rotated to sit in front of another girl, while the girls stayed seated. Each player was given a speed dating card to check yes or no to whether they'd like to see that person again.

Ask people going into a round of speed dating what they're looking for in a mate, and usually they will say they are looking for things like a sense of humor, kindness, good looks, ambition. But if you examine their cards after they have speed dated, you find that what people say they want, and what they actually go for, can be very different. But why?

The answer is the X factor. It is commonly known as chemistry or vibe. Even if two speed daters have everything in common on paper, this X factor needs to be present for them to want to date. It is, in large part, a physical attraction involving pheromones that mesh well together.

Whatever you call it, it's something that can't be predicted. But ultimately it's the most important factor when it comes to wanting to see someone again.

THAT NIGHT I CHECK the speed dating e-mail account to see if any of the e-mails have bounced back. I'm surprised when I see how many people have replied to the e-mail.

I open the first one.

Thanks, it was fun, but are you sure Stephanie or Angie didn't check me off?

I open another one. Only two matches? Could you recount it?

Another one. Please take a look again—I'm sure Shamar checked me off.

And the list goes on. To my surprise, a lot of people expected they'd be checked off by people who didn't check them off. I double-check each of the cards just in case, but I don't find any mistakes.

Hmm. This must mean that people often don't get the *real* vibe the other person is giving off. Maybe they see what they want to see. Or maybe the other speed daters were being especially nice because they knew they weren't going to check them off.

I open an e-mail from Evgeney Vraslov:

Thank you for letting me play. Nobody checked me. Did I do something wrong? Could I try again next year?

My heart breaks for him. Poor Evgeney. I reply:

Hi Evgeney,

A lot of people didn't make matches, so don't worry about it—you didn't do anything wrong. If we do it again next year, I'll let you know. In the meantime, there's this Web site called the Oracle of Dating you might want to check out. You don't have to pay to read the blog. See you at school!

Kayla ☺

I'm not sure I did the right thing by mentioning the Oracle, but there might be information on the Web site that could help him, especially since I recently wrote a blog for guys called *What Girls Are Looking For.* Note to self: add another blog or two that could help Evgeney. One of them would definitely have to be on fashion because if Evgeney is ever going to find a girl, he'll need a full makeover.

As I'm replying to the other e-mails, an instant message pops up for the Oracle.

LostGirl: I'm really depressed.
Oracle: What's wrong?
LostGirl: There's this guy I really like and I think he likes me, too.
Oracle: And?
LostGirl: He's not Indian. My parents will freak out if I date a guy who isn't Indian.

Viv would be able to relate to this girl! Her parents are the same way.

the oracle of dating

Oracle: Are you sure they would freak out? Do you think after a while they might come to accept him?

LostGirl: My parents are very traditional. A while ago I asked them what they'd do if I wanted to date a guy who isn't Indian, and they said there was no way they'd let me. I love my parents and I know they want what's best for me. But I think they might be wrong about this. I just don't know!

Oracle: Do you like this guy enough to upset your parents?

LostGirl: I don't want to upset them but I like this guy so much. I kept telling myself that he didn't like me back, but then we did this speed dating thing at school, and I was the only one he checked off. So now I'm thinking he must like me.

Oh my God! I'm talking to Viv!

Oracle: Did you check him off?

LostGirl: No. How could I?

Oracle: Maybe you could find someone to talk to your parents for you—a teacher or a relative.

LostGirl: All my relatives would agree with them. I don't want to tell a teacher this stuff. I haven't even told my friends.

Oracle: Do you *really* want to date this guy?

LostGirl: Yes, I really do.

Oracle: Then date him. Follow your heart. Life is too short not to be with the one you want. Your parents are from a

Allison van Diepen

different generation and a different country. They will realize sooner or later that you're going to forge your own path.

LostGirl: If I date him, should I tell them, or keep him a secret?

Oracle: That depends. If you think there's a chance they could accept it, it may be worth taking the risk. But if you think they will definitely be against it, then you might have to date him without them knowing.

I hope I'm handling this right, but hey, they can't rule her life forever.

LostGirl: You're right, Oracle. It's my life.

Oracle: Yes, it is. Keep in mind that you're very young (I assume you're in high school), so even if you date a guy who isn't Indian, that doesn't mean you're going to marry one.

LostGirl: Actually, I don't know if my parents agree with me dating at all. They didn't date before they got married. They just met a few times. Relatives introduced them. But I'm going to follow my heart, like you said. Thank you, Oracle. You're very wise.

Oracle: Socrates said the wisest people know that they are not wise at all. As the Oracle, I listen, and learn.

LostGirl: Well, I think you're great. Thanks so much for your help.

Oracle: Good luck.

LostGirl: Bye, Oracle.

I can't believe I took five bucks from one of my best friends to give her advice I should be giving her anyway! I'll have to buy her a latte to make up for it.

Now I'm faced with a decision. Do I tell Viv the truth about who I am and reveal that I know her problem? Or should I say nothing?

Damn it, I have to tell her before this goes any further. I pick up the phone and speed-dial her number.

"Hello?"

"Hey, Viv."

"Hi. I'm on the other line with Max. Can I call you back?"

"Sure. Max, huh? That's awesome."

"We're just friends." But her giggle gives her away. "Talk to you later."

"Bye, Viv."

Wow. If I didn't know the Oracle's impact before, I totally know it now.

eight

SPEED DATING IS THE *only* topic of conversation in the halls on Monday. Everybody's asking me if there is going to be another one. I answer, "Maybe next year." A bunch of people come up to me asking for their results—I tell them nicely that I don't have a photographic memory so they need to check their e-mail.

My heart beats in my throat as I walk into fourth-period earth science class. I've convinced myself that I'll know within a second of meeting Jared's eyes whether what he wrote on the speed dating card has anything to do with me.

"Hey." He must not have heard me, because he doesn't look up—he's doodling as usual.

A few seconds later, he looks up and smiles at me. "Hi, Kayla."

And that's all of our interaction for the entire class. Not

that we could really talk if we wanted to, with Ms. Goff blabbering away, but he's not even glancing in my direction.

Something inside me deflates.

I'm a total idiot. I've built a fantasy around being the mysterious Girl #13 on his dating card. What did I expect? That he'd confess his adoration when I came into class? That he would look at me with eyes full of longing?

I should be glad that he's not interested. Then I won't be tempted to break my rule, which is in place to save me from heartbreak and humiliation. It's just an attraction, I remind myself. It'll fade in time.

When the bell rings, Jared says over his shoulder, "See ya in art." And I try not to acknowledge that my heart flutters with anticipation.

I head to the caf, buy my lunch and find my friends involved in a morbid discussion about death.

"Dying of hypothermia is supposed to be awesome," Ryan is saying. "On TLC, there was this guy who died of hypothermia and they resuscitated him. He said it was like falling into a deep, cozy sleep."

"I'd rather die in a cozy sleep than in a snowdrift," I put in.

Viv says, "There's this ad on the subway—I think it's a beer ad—that says, *May you get shot by a jealous lover when you're ninety-five.* I don't think it's funny."

Ryan laughs. "You get the point, don't you? They're

saying if you've got a lover when you're ninety-five, you're doing great."

"I know what they're getting at, I just don't like it. My grandmother is ninety-two. If anyone shot her, I'd kill them."

I think I'd better change the subject. "Did you hear about that minister down south who was preaching about heaven and suddenly dropped dead? I asked my mom if she'd like to die that way and she said no, it would be too traumatic for the congregation. She'd like to die in church but not until after she retires. And she'd want to keel over in her pew during the benediction so it wouldn't interrupt the service."

"Enough about this death stuff," Ryan says. "Let's talk about what we all want to do *before* we die."

"Lose my virginity to Mike P.!" Sharese declares.

"What's this about losing your virginity?" We look up to see Max McIver with his lunch tray. "Can I join you guys?"

We nod. He circles to the other side of the table to slide in beside Viv. They exchange a glance and she drops her eyes, a blush rising under her skin. Max's gaze lingers on her for several moments before he starts eating his lunch. Sharese and Ryan seem surprised.

I look away, smiling to myself.

"GOOD SHOW FRIDAY night," Jared says.

"Thanks again for coming."

"Wasn't a bad time."

"I noticed you didn't, um, make any matches."

"I went as a favor to you. I wasn't looking for a match." He picks up a pencil and starts doodling intricate little boxes. "Did you play one of the rounds?"

"No. I was focused on making sure everything went smoothly." I dare a glance at him. What I see is friendly warmth, not burning heat. I wish I'd never admitted to myself that I'm attracted to him. It makes it oh so awkward to be near him.

Am I imagining it, or is he suddenly looking a little awkward himself? He clears his throat. "I've got something to ask you." He reaches into his knapsack.

OMG, is he going to do it right here, right now? Tell me I'm Girl #13? I seriously might pass out.

He puts a crumpled blue flyer in front of me, smoothing it out. "My band is playing Friday night at the Vox. You should come."

"Sure." I say it too quickly. I should really be saying, *I'll try.* But I know that I'll more than try. After he did me a favor by going to speed dating, the least I can do is show up to support his band. But mostly, I'd love to see him play. It's universally known that a guy playing a guitar is sexy, and Jared already has a head start in that area. After he plays, maybe we'll hang out. Dance together. Who knows?

I can see my no-dating-until-college rule flashing in my brain like a neon sign.

"Could you bring your friends, too? As many friends

as possible? It's our first time playing a gig at this place and we need to show them we can get a good crowd if we're ever going to play there again."

"Of course. I'll bring people." And now I'm not so sure if I've been personally invited, or just recruited to bring people. He smiles at me, quick and bright like a camera flash, but I'm not sure why anymore.

"Do I need ID?"

"They usually don't card people. Do you have a fake?"

I think back to the laminated student card from my birthday. "Yeah, but it's not very good."

"Bring it just in case. You should be fine." Another smile, and there it is again, that fluttering in my chest. I wonder if he's feeling the same vibe I'm feeling. But thinking back to the speed dating results, I realize he probably isn't. The proof is all those e-mails from people thinking someone had checked them off when they hadn't.

Attraction, apparently, is often accompanied by delusion.

Either way, I'll show up Friday night. After his band plays, he'll either pay attention to me or he won't, and that will tell me once and for all if I'm Girl #13.

And if it really is me, then maybe, just maybe, I'll think about breaking my rule.

FRIDAY CAN'T SEEM TO ARRIVE fast enough, but there's plenty of excitement in the meantime—namely, Viv and Max's budding romance. Although they're avoiding all PDA, I could tell right away that they'd made the step from friendship to couplehood. Viv told us officially on Wednesday that she's dating Max on the down-low, and that we're all strictly forbidden to say anything to anyone about it.

Viv didn't call me back Sunday night, so I never ended up telling her that I am the Oracle. And since she hasn't contacted the Oracle again, I figure there's no need to.

As I count the hours until Friday night, I write several new blogs for my Web site, including one that could be helpful to Evgeney.

How to Be a Romantic Hero

Guys, do you ever wonder why girls are overlooking you? What is it about you that puts you in the "friend" category, and not the "boyfriend" one?

What you need is to take a hint from what many girls are reading—yes, romance novels (of the teen or adult variety). To save you some time, I will describe some characteristics of the romantic hero girls are dreaming about.

He has an aura of strength and masculinity about him. Even if he's not big and strong, he's got something to replace it: he's smart, an expert in his field. He's powerful, a leader. He's confident and doesn't need rescuing.

He's ambitious. Life is something he takes by the horns! He doesn't wait for things to happen, he makes them happen.

He's gorgeous. No, he's odd-looking, even scarred. Here's the great thing: it doesn't matter. If you're sexy and masculine, you don't need to look like Harrison on *Glamour Girl*. (In fact, there is, lately, a distinct movement *against* pretty boys.)

He's well-put-together. Or at least, he's not a fashion disaster. Don't let your mom or grandma dress you unless they're in touch with current styles. If you're clueless, check out some catalogs and copy the styles you see there. Or better yet, go into a store and have someone working there dress you.

How should you act? It's all about confidence. Are you shy? Don't act it. Instead, act reserved, quietly confident, like you're fascinated by your own thoughts. And don't come across as eager. Be calm, totally zen.

Good luck!

The O.

JASON IS ONE OF A CURIOUS breed of Manhattan guys who can't accept that he is living in the city and shouldn't have a huge dog in his tiny apartment. In this case, the dog is a blubbering Great Dane.

Tracey met him at a friend's dinner party and calls me

the next day, cautiously excited. "This guy's amazing, Kayla! He's an analyst for Goldman Sachs. Went to Brown. Says he's a chocolate snob. I hope he calls."

He does call, and they have a great first date at a Thai restaurant. Jason is a vegetarian who eats fish, and they split a double order of shrimp pad thai.

For their second date, Jason invites her over for a home-cooked meal. Tracey is impressed—he's handsome, witty and a passionate chef! She always felt that she deserved a man who is talented in the kitchen as well as the bedroom.

She arrives a fashionable fifteen minutes late, having dropped fifty bucks for a bottle of red. She knows she looks great in a new white halter dress.

The moment she walks in the door, Jason shouts, "Down, Buddy, down!"

But the dog is already on top of her, jumping up and shoving her back with two forceful paws. Tracey stumbles back, handing off the wine bottle. The dog weighs more than she does.

Jason grabs the dog's collar. "*Down, boy.* Sorry, he's just being playful. He's only a puppy."

That is a puppy? Tracey thinks. He's going to get bigger?

Deciding to be a good sport, Tracey smoothes her dress and pets the dog. Buddy tries to jump up again, but Jason has a firm hold on him. "Would you let him smell you for a minute? Come a little closer. If he can smell you, he'll calm down."

Tracey takes a step closer. Hopefully Buddy will be soothed by Estée Lauder's Pleasures.

Suddenly Buddy breaks away from Jason and sticks his nose right in Tracey's crotch.

Tracey gives a horrified shriek.

"Easy, he's just getting familiar with you."

Tracey shudders, bearing it for a minute before Jason pulls the dog back. She feels violated. What right does this dog have to stick his face in between her legs?

"I'd better get to the kitchen before something burns. Have a seat. Let me open this wine."

She sits on a bar stool. Out of the corner of her eye, she's surveying Buddy's movements. She notices a tear in one of her nylons from his initial attack.

Jason, of course, is focused on cooking. He opens the wine and pours them each a glass, and comments that it's fantastic wine, and she says it's Napa Valley.

The wine and the delicious aromas of the meal have a calming effect on Tracey. She glances over at Buddy, feeling sorry for the poor thing. It can't be easy being such a big dog in a small one-bedroom. Perhaps she shouldn't be angry that he tore her nylons. He surely didn't mean to.

An explosive farting sound tears through the apartment. Jason laughs. "Holy shit! Buddy's never done that in front of company before. Sorry!"

"It's okay," says Tracey, all compassion. Poor Buddy

suffers from gastrointestinal issues on top of everything else.

And then the smell hits her.

She waves a hand in front of her face. "Can I open a window?"

"Sure."

A few minutes later, they sit down to a lovely, candlelit dinner. The only flaw? Buddy's flatulence kicks into high gear.

Jason can't stop laughing. "I took him for a walk earlier and caught him nibbling on some roadkill. Must've made him sick."

"I see." Tracey's food suddenly becomes less appetizing. The evening is going downhill fast. She hopes dinner will be done quickly so they can get out of this place and away from this dog.

But the worst is yet to come.

As Jason is clearing the dinner plates, Buddy jumps up to get some scraps.

The next event occurs as if in slow motion.

With a huge paw, Buddy slaps a plate out of Jason's hand. The plate does a backward flip and lands in Tracey's lap.

Tracey lifts the plate and looks down in horror. Tomato sauce all over her white dress!

"Shit, sorry." Jason comes at her with a napkin as

Buddy jumps around the room gleefully. "I'll get some club soda."

"It won't work. I need to get this to a dry cleaner right away. There's an all-night one near my place. I'll be back in an hour."

"All right."

She hesitates before leaving. He's not going to offer to pay?

She closes the door as Jason begins to play with his dog.

Tracey never goes back.

And Jason never calls.

"WOW, KAYLA." Ryan's eyes widen when he sees me in the subway station. "Somebody actually made an effort!"

"Yeah, so?"

"So I love it! You're definitely picking up tonight."

The truth? I hope he's right. But I haven't told him or any of the others about my crush on Jared. I just told them we should go to see this band and lots of people from school will be there. Hopefully, by the end of the night, they'll see me getting cozy with the hot guitarist…

We meet up with Amy, Chad, Sharese, Viv and Max at the Astor Place station around nine-thirty. They all comment on how good I look, making me wonder how bad I look the rest of the time. But it's true, I put a lot of effort in tonight, not the least of which is overcoming my fear of a red-hot flatiron in order to straighten my hair. I also put on makeup, my cutest jeans and a silver top. I know the silver is a bit of a fashion risk, but I also know that it brings out the sparkle in my eyes. It's all about confidence, anyway.

When we get to the Vox on Avenue B, there's already a lineup. A bouncer is standing beside the door checking IDs.

"I thought you said they didn't check here." Sharese frowns. "They're checking almost everyone."

"New management, maybe." But I'm not feeling good about this.

"Chad should go first," Amy says. "He's got his brother's ID."

I can tell Amy's hyped to get in. I must have sold her on the event. That, or she saw a few seniors go in and she doesn't want them to get ahead of her.

We're out there about twenty minutes before Chad's up to bat. The bouncer pauses for a second with his ID, then lets him in. My heart is pounding. I absolutely *have to* get in.

Amy's turn. The bouncer hardly looks at her ID. She's in.

I'm up next. I hand over my ID, trying to look casual. Meanwhile my head resounds with the thuds of my pulse. Bam. Bam.

The bouncer stares at me, squinting. I look up at him, trying not to be intimidated by his stare.

"I'm supposed to believe you're twenty-one?" He looks me up and down. "Yeah, right. Show me some other ID to prove it."

"Um…" I do some fumbling in my handbag. It's too

small to hold a wallet, so all my ID cards and money are loose. Then he reaches in and snatches my real student ID.

"Michaela Cruickshank, Midwood high school. Twenty-one and still in high school, huh?"

My face burns. A bunch of people are laughing and snickering, including some seniors from our school. I want to walk away, but the bouncer holds my eyes, his face contorting. "You're a junior? I'd have pegged you for a freshman. I'm sick of you kiddies always trying to get in here. Why shouldn't I call the police?"

I feel my lips tremble. *Stay calm. Everyone is staring at you.* If I weren't so freaked out by a man twice my size shouting at me, I might mention that half of the people in line are underage. As it is, I'm trying not to cower under the menace in his eyes.

"Well? I asked you a question."

"I'm sorry. I just thought…"

"You didn't think, *that* was the problem. Don't you know we could get fined and shut down if the cops find kiddies like you in there? You wanna run this place out of business?"

I shake my head.

"Then you and your little friends better take off."

I nod. Ryan and Sharese grab my hands and we run up the block, Viv and Max right behind us.

Once the bar is out of sight, we stop running. "I can't believe that guy!" Ryan gasps for breath. "What an asshole!"

Sharese looks traumatized. "I thought he was really going to call the police on us."

"I wouldn't have said I was with you guys," I tell them.

"It doesn't matter—he saw we were all together," Ryan says.

"What about Chad and Amy?" Viv asks. "They're already inside."

"I'll text her." Ryan takes out his phone.

"Let's find a café or something." Viv puts an arm around me. "It's okay, Kayla. You can see the band play another time."

But it wasn't okay. What's Jared going to think—that I didn't bother to show up? That I don't live up to my word? If I had his number, I'd call him and explain what happened. But it looks like I'll have to wait until Monday.

No, it wasn't okay at all.

We hop a train back to Park Slope and head to Ozzie's café on Seventh Avenue, one of our favorite hangouts. It's quiet tonight, so there are plenty of seats. The five of us get drinks, then squeeze around a table.

I tell myself that this isn't bad, it's even kind of cozy. My soy latte, sprinkled with cinnamon, is tasty and not overly foamy. But the thought that I could be seeing Jared on stage right now is a bitter pill to swallow. How will I ever have the chance to find out if I'm Girl #13? I have this queasy feeling in the pit of my stomach, this feeling that tells me I've lost my chance.

Ryan is dominating the conversation with tales of his annoying little sister, but only Sharese seems to be paying attention. Viv and Max are obviously holding hands under the table, or playing footsie, or both. I catch sight of their eye contact, and it's hot, so hot it's a little uncomfortable. Sharese and Ryan don't seem to notice.

I wonder if Jared and I would be like that, eager to be close, eager to be alone. Something tells me that Jared isn't the type to play games for very long, that he'd let a girl know if he wanted to be alone with her. At the thought, a quiver goes through me. I remember the flash in his eyes in the school bus when I practically rolled onto his lap. That was real, mutual attraction. It had to be.

Viv lets out a little yelp, as if Max did something to her under the table. "Sorry, guys—it's nothing!" She manages to hide her smile, but Max is less successful. I don't try to hide mine. It's great to see Viv and Max together at last. Happy endings do happen… with a little help from the Oracle.

nine

OR MAYBE NOT.

The next morning Amy's call wakes me up.

"You missed a mind-blowing show last night, Kayla. Sorry you didn't get in. I heard it was pretty embarrassing."

"Freaking humiliating."

"I hope you don't mind that Chad and I stayed to see the band."

"I don't blame you. Was there a big crowd?"

"Oh, yeah. Half the school was there. And Jared Stewart was looking good, honey. You should've seen it—Brooke was all over him after the show. They even left together."

I feel like I've been socked in the gut.

"Funny, isn't it? I wouldn't have pictured them hooking up. She's so priss and he's so...alternative. But it's true, he was sexy up there. Can you believe we thought he was gay because he didn't check her off on his speed dating card?"

I find my voice. "I never thought that."

"Okay, fine, *I* did. But here's my question. Why would Brooke go after the one guy who didn't check her off at speed dating? I would've thought she'd be pissed off at him."

You don't need to be the Oracle of Dating to figure it out. "You want who you can't have. Brooke was probably more attracted to him after he didn't check her off."

"So he was playing the old hard-to-get strategy."

"I doubt it was a strategy." Or was it? Had Jared invited Brooke to the show, too?

We talk a little while longer, but the more I hear about the show, the more depressed I get. By the time I hang up, I feel downright ill. The thought of Jared and Brooke together makes me want to throw up. Why would he go for her when he wrote on his speed dating card that she was a fake?

Maybe it's only physical. Maybe she'll sleep with him. Everyone knows that she and Declan were doing it like…like rabid rabbits.

I squeeze my eyes shut, but it doesn't block the mental image of Jared and Brooke getting hot and heavy. Ick. Ew. No, thank you. I'm not going to think about it.

What's wrong with me? What do I care if Jared's sleeping with Brooke, or anyone else, for that matter?

Because I want Jared for myself, that's why. And not just in a physical way—in the boyfriendly way. I was going to break my no-dating-until-college rule for him, and thought last night would be the turning point for us. Instead I didn't get in, and Brooke did.

I lost my chance.

I have no business feeling sorry for myself. If I'd wanted to be with Jared, I should've made a move weeks ago. Instead I'd stupidly clung to my rule, and focused on everything about him that didn't make him my ideal boyfriend.

Maybe I'm better off. Maybe there's no way we would've lasted. But how can I know that for sure? What if he was the guy who would've lasted, the high school crush who turns out to be a soul mate?

I'd thought my rule would save me from heartbreak, but I was wrong.

I SPEND THE WEEKEND feeling sorry for my sorry-ass self. I can't help it. It's so unfair that I didn't get into the club when most of the underaged people did. It's so unfair that Jared left with Brooke. Things can't get any worse.

When I wake up Monday morning, I tell myself to stop being ridiculous and get it together. After showering and brushing my teeth, I stare into the bathroom mirror, preparing myself to encounter Jared by schooling my face in expressions of lightness and indifference. I decide an aloof smile is the way to go.

When I walk up to my locker, I see that Sharese has her arm around Viv.

"What's going on?"

Sharese's eyes are grave. "Her parents found out about Max."

Viv raises her head. "My mom found a note he wrote me. They're furious that I lied to them. I'm grounded for…forever."

"I'm so sorry, Viv." She has no idea how sorry. This is *my* fault. I'm the one who gave her the advice.

"I broke up with Max over the phone last night. It can never work with my parents in the way. I made a stupid mistake. I should never have tried to date him."

Sharese squeezes Viv to her side. "Don't blame yourself. You were being true to your feelings. You can't regret that."

"I've hurt Max and my parents. How can I not regret that? I knew this was going to happen. I just knew it. But I didn't want to see it. I was in a dreamworld."

She had reason to be in a dreamworld because she was in love. That's why she came to me, the Oracle of Dating, for rational advice. And I failed her.

I can't believe I failed her.

The bell rings, forcing us to separate. As I sit in class, the weight of the truth is pressing down on me. I need to tell Viv that I'm the Oracle of Dating and that I'm responsible for screwing up her life. At least if I tell her, she'll know it's my fault and she can stop blaming herself.

She might hate me. I could lose one of the best friends I've ever had. And if I do, I deserve it.

Classes go by in a blur. I keep running over the advice I

gave her. I got it so wrong. The Oracle told her what she wanted to hear—*follow your heart and all will be well.* But the Oracle is supposed to be smarter than that. She's supposed to give a sensible assessment of the situation. She's supposed to explore the problem intellectually before giving an answer. Instead I got swept up in the excitement of Viv and Max getting together and gave her stupid advice.

What was I thinking? Culturally sensitive questions should never be answered so flippantly. I *know* that. And yet somehow, because I was dealing with a friend, I acted more like opinionated Kayla than impartial Oracle. Damn myself!

In earth science, I see Jared, and I remember that I'm upset he got together with Brooke. Suddenly I feel even worse than I did a few minutes ago, if that's humanly possible.

I say, "Hey."

Jared gives me a nod, but his eyes are guarded. For a minute I think he's going to ask me where I was Friday night, but he doesn't. It hits me that he didn't even notice my absence. He probably only asked me to go so I'd bring people. And now that he's cozy with Brooke, he doesn't have to bother with me. He's got a VIP pass to popularity.

But I really don't care about that right now. I have bigger problems than Jared. I've hurt Viv, and it's killing me.

A horrible thought hits me. How many people's lives have I screwed up by giving bad advice?

I used to think I was doing something good for this world by being the Oracle of Dating, but I'm not sure

anymore. I'm not a licensed therapist. I have no creden-
tials except a belief in my own good judgment. What was
I doing giving advice?

I realize that I have no choice but to take down the Web
site.

Snap! My pen goes flying, hitting the wall near Jared's
head. He hands it to me, eyes narrowed. "You okay?"

"Yeah, fine."

He frowns, but lowers his head to focus on his doodling.

My eyes linger on him. Did my crush on Jared cause
me to lose my edge?

Or did I ever have an edge at all?

LUNCHTIME IN THE CAF is excruciating. Viv is in a stupor
of sadness and we're falling all over ourselves to comfort
her, but it's not having any effect. Max is across the caf
sitting with his friends, glancing at Viv with the most ex-
quisite longing.

I'm tempted to spill the beans all over the lunch table
and tell everyone that I'm the Oracle and it's my fault. But
I manage to resist. Facing Viv will be hard enough without
my other friends questioning me, too. If Viv wants to
reveal my secret to them, that's up to her.

I'd like to get Viv alone to get this off my chest, but I
doubt it will happen with everyone coddling her. Since
she's grounded and has to report home right after school,
my only chance is to call her—if she's allowed to take calls.

She hasn't been grounded in recent memory, so I don't know how strict her parents will be.

After lunch is English class, which is too hideously boring to give me an escape from my thoughts. Then it's art class, and I'm tempted to work at another desk so I won't have to deal with Jared; but then, he might clue in that I'm upset about him leaving with Brooke on Friday night. I don't have time for Jared heartsickness right now. He could've left with ten groupies, for all I care.

He comes up to the desk, putting down his books. "How's it going, Kayla?"

I wish he wouldn't use my name. It's well-known that everyone likes to hear their name. I know my damned name.

I shrug. "Okay. You?"

"Good."

Is he gloating or something?

Ms. Gerstad starts the lesson, and I pretend to pay attention. Out of the corner of my eye I see Jared writing on a piece of paper. He slides it in front of me.

I didn't see you there Friday night.

So he did notice. Not that it matters now.

I wonder if there's any point in telling him what happened. Since he obviously wasn't broken up over my absence, I won't bother to recount my humiliation.

I write back, *Sorry. I wanted to but it didn't work out. How'd it go?*

Great.

I bet it went great. A successful show and the school's most popular girl for a groupie.

Yeah, I'm a sore loser. But I'm having a very bad day.

We're working with charcoal today. After Ms. Gerstad gives the instructions, we grab our materials and get started. Jared and I chat a little as we work, but it's small talk, nothing real.

I've got a knot in my stomach the size of Texas whenever I think of what I've done to Viv. I'm the cause of my friend's broken heart and damaged relationship with her parents. It's downright nauseating.

Jared puts his hand on mine, charcoal smearing my hand. A frisson of warmth goes through me, and I look up at him. But he's not looking at me, he's nudging his chin toward the doorway.

Viv is waving to get my attention, a closed-fisted, tissue-clutching wave. I ask Gerstad for the bathroom pass.

In the hall, Viv's eyes are shiny with tears. "Max left a note in my locker. He wants to keep dating in secret. But I can't, Kayla. I can't!"

I don't know what to say. I want to cry, too.

We go sit in the courtyard behind the school. It's the unofficial smoking area, and the ground is covered with cigarette butts. The sun hasn't come out, leaving the sky a dull, gloomy gray. Just the way Viv and I feel. Chilly

October weather has caused the leaves to shrivel up and fall in crinkled, colorless masses.

"I'm cutting class, Kayla. Can you believe that? I've never cut a class in my life. I don't even recognize myself anymore."

"Give yourself a break. You have a lot to deal with right now. Of course you should cut class."

Great, I'm giving her more destructive advice. I might as well suggest she kill the pain with alcohol and drugs.

"I have something to tell you." I hesitate. Maybe I shouldn't. Maybe I'm just adding to her troubles by dumping this on her. Maybe—

"Well, what is it?"

"I'm the Oracle of Dating."

"It's *you?*"

I nod, bracing myself for an explosion.

"That's cool!"

"Huh?" Her heartbreak must have caused temporary insanity. I guess she's not getting the implication of what I just told her. "Do you know what this means?"

"Uh, no, what does it mean?"

"It's my fault this happened. I gave you horrible advice. I'm so sorry. I felt bad giving you advice in the first place without you knowing it was me. I called you afterward to come clean, but you were on the phone with Max. And once you guys starting dating, I figured you didn't need to know."

"I haven't been blaming the Oracle for my situation. I knew the Oracle was just telling me what I wanted to hear."

"The Oracle—I mean, *I* don't usually tell people what they want to hear. I try to give good advice. But I wanted to see you and Max together so much that my personal feelings got in the way. I was totally culturally insensitive and unprofessional. I don't feel I deserve to be the Oracle. I'm taking the Web site down after school today."

"That's silly. Your Web site is awesome. I knew it wasn't some old guy running it! The advice always felt real. Why didn't you tell all of us in the first place?"

I lower my head. I have a dozen possible answers to that one. "I don't know. I guess I was afraid you'd all laugh at the idea that I could be giving dating advice when I haven't dated much myself."

"I wouldn't have laughed. You're smart, Kayla. You're a thinker."

"Not when I was giving you advice, apparently. You have every right to be mad at me. I'm mad at myself."

"I'm not mad at you. I think it's cool that you're the Oracle. I just wish *I'd* reacted differently to this situation. I've let everyone down and I don't know if my parents will ever trust me again."

"They will. I'm sure they will."

I'm doing it again. I'm telling her what I think she wants to hear.

But the look on her face says she's not buying it this time. "I hope they will. Someday."

WHEN I GET HOME from school, I go right to my computer. The screen fills with the pink and blue bubbles of the oracleofdating.com. Looking at the results of the latest poll, it turns out that seventy-four percent of respondents said they'd prefer to be stranded on a desert island with all three Jonas brothers instead of just one. Hmm. Does that mean most girls feel that the rules of monogamy don't apply when you're dealing with brothers? That's a blog topic in itself.

I take a deep breath. There won't be any more blogs, polls or anything else. By giving Viv such terrible advice, I broke the cardinal rule of people in the helping professions: do no harm. I don't want to mess up anyone else's life like I did Viv's. Just because she's kind enough not to blame me doesn't change the truth: the Oracle of Dating failed.

With a simple click, I take the Web site off-line. And now, when anyone goes to oracleofdating.com, they will see a generic yahoo business page.

I feel an emptiness in my chest, as if with that one click, I took away my life's purpose.

ten

OVER THE NEXT FEW DAYS, something becomes painfully clear: I don't know what to do with myself when I'm not being the Oracle. Sure, I have homework, the Hellhole, reading Ellen's steamy historical romance novels and talking on the phone with friends to keep me busy. But I don't feel like myself. I feel lost.

Every day at school I see the sadness in Viv's eyes and my heart breaks for her. Her parents are grounding her for six weeks, which is both cruel and unusual, since I've never heard of anyone being grounded for more than a month. That means she won't be able to emerge again until late November, and that feels like an eternity away. But worse than the grounding is the tension between her and her parents, which I know is tearing her up inside.

If she were mad at me, maybe I'd have a chance at paying the penance and eventually getting over my guilt. But she's as sweet to me as ever and doesn't want me to shoulder any of the blame. Somehow that makes me feel worse. She refuses to punish me, so I feel I should punish myself.

But I probably don't need to punish myself, since the universe is doing a good job of it already. Every day, Brooke and Jared appear to be getting closer, cuddlier, to the point that I hardly see one without the other. By Thursday morning it's clear that Jared and Brooke are together. She's at his locker, cooing over him, ruffling his hair, practically groping him. Jared plays it cool, but I'm sure he's eating up all the attention. And why shouldn't he? The hottest girl in school is all over him, and his reputation has turned from *not*tie to hottie overnight.

With his newfound fame, I half expect him to ignore my existence, but Jared isn't like that. I wish he were, because then I could hate him. But the fact is, Jared hasn't let his fame go to his head, and I can't hate him at all.

I just feel…*longing*. It's hard to get over a crush when I have to see him every day and smell his cologne. And seeing him and Brooke together drives a stake through my heart.

Not to be overly dramatic, but you know what I mean.

FRIDAY NIGHT I ELECT to stay home. I'm tired and depressed and want to be alone. I spend the evening sitting on my bed reading. I've put the hot historical romance novel on hold in favor of the tragic vampire romance Viv insisted I read. I understand why she loves it. It reminds her of her situation with Max. The romance that can't be.

This book is making me downright weepy. As I read, I picture Jared as the brooding vampire. He looks just the way he does now, with those dreamy blue eyes and almost-black hair, but he's pale, with long incisors and a black cape. And when he looks at me, I feel his raging passion.

I can't help going to the computer and writing:

Lovesickness: You Want Who You Can't Have

Think of the best romance novel you've ever read, or your favorite romantic TV show or movie. Why are these stories so compelling that you could cry just thinking about them?

It's because these romances are impossible.

These days it seems many of these love stories are supernatural. Your feisty heroine has fallen for a vampire who can never grow old with her or fit into her world. Your lovesick hero falls for a fairy who can never be his. Your heroine falls for a ghost who lives across the chasm of time, across a void she can't cross.

In other cases, the conflicts separating the lovers are all too human. Like when lovers come from different cultures or religions, and their families won't let them be together. Or like two people falling in love when their countries are at war.

I know lovesickness. I know how painful it can be. Even if your loved one is not a vampire, even if he's that boy in class—if you can't have him, it hurts. It aches.

Some of the worst lovesickness is from love that isn't returned. Maybe he never really noticed you. Maybe he chose someone else over you—say, a popular blonde with large breasts. If you dwell on this, if you listen to sappy ballads about impossible love, you will hurt even more.

Lovesickness, that painful longing, has no real cure. In some cases, time and distance may help you move on. But the memories remain. Memories of a love that was never realized—or a what-if that will always haunt you.

It's not a bad article. It's definitely from the heart. But with the Web site down, I can't post it. So I delete it, and feel a sense of loss all over again.

If I'd gotten into the bar that night, would Jared have gravitated toward me instead of Brooke? If I'd worked up the courage to ask him out a few weeks ago, would we have had a chance?

The truth is, Jared is a *what-if* that will always haunt me.

AROUND TEN THAT NIGHT, I go to the kitchen in search of a snack. Erland is in the living room reading, his glasses perched on the edge of his nose. Mom isn't around. She has a Friday-night Bible study, which to me is just wrong.

"How are you feeling?" Erland's voice startles me as I'm pouring soy milk into my cereal. I'm used to him being quiet most of the time, a bookish ghost in my peripheral vision.

"I'm fine, why?"

"Usually you see your friends on Friday evenings."

"There wasn't much going on."

He's looking at me over his reading glasses. "You have not seemed yourself all week."

I'm surprised he noticed. But it's not like I can tell him how I screwed up as the Oracle, since he didn't even know I was the Oracle. And I don't feel like telling him that I'm upset because of a guy. I doubt the concept would register in his theological brain.

"It's been a stressful week."

A bushy brow goes up, as if he doesn't believe me. Does he really expect me to tell him the truth? We hardly ever talk.

"Saturn is square Jupiter," he says. "That might explain whatever events have troubled you."

"Excuse me?"

He beckons me over. I leave my cereal on the counter and go sit beside him on the couch. He shows me the book he's reading, which is full of numbers and symbols. "This is an ephemeris. It gives the planetary positions on any given date."

"You're into astrology?" I don't get it. Erland doesn't have a New Age bone in his body.

"It is an ancient science."

"But is it cool with, you know, the people at the seminary?"

"They do not know, and I hope you will not say anything. I am not ashamed of my interest, but some of my colleagues are not open-minded when it comes to the ancient sciences."

Whoa. The Swede is a rebel. "I won't tell. Does Mom know?"

"Yes. I warned her that there is a strongly negative aspect this week—Saturn square Jupiter. So I wouldn't be surprised if things did not go smoothly at the Bible study."

"So if I've been having problems this week, it could be because of this aspect?"

"The causal nature of it is difficult to identify, but yes, this would be a time when conflicts arise. It would be a poor time to make financial investments, for instance."

"At least I don't have to worry about that. I have no money to invest, anyway. Does it relate to personal stuff, too?"

"Oh, yes. At a time like this, interpersonal relationships are often strained. It wouldn't be a time to resolve a conflict with a partner, or ask a boss for a raise. Better to wait until the aspect passes in a few days."

This is seriously cool. If I'd known Erland was an astrologer, I could've given love horoscopes. Too late for that now. "You're right about this week. Things have been pretty screwed up. It felt like a lot of bad things happened at once, you know?"

"That makes sense. However, negative aspects are necessary in order for positive ones to occur. There must be balance in space as well as on earth."

I try to think of how Viv's situation could turn positive. Or how I could be happy again without being the Oracle. Or how I could ever stand seeing Jared and Brooke together. But I can't.

"Things will resolve themselves one way or another, Kayla. All things pass, good and bad. All events have lessons."

"Yeah, but we can't take back the mistakes we make."

"If you made a mistake, you will have learned from it. And perhaps it will set in motion other processes which will ultimately lead to karmic resolution."

Now I'm starting to get confused, because I thought Buddhists talked about karma, not Swedish Christian theologians. Still, I have to admit, the Swede is cooler than I thought.

THE NEXT AFTERNOON, Amy calls to tell me we're going to a keg party tonight. I don't argue. I need to get out. If I stay home wallowing another night, I'll just get more depressed. I only wish Viv had the option of going out, too.

"Whose party is it?" I ask.

"Dave from the soccer team. He told Chad to bring whoever he wants."

Which is as good as an invitation. Why not? I have nothing else to do.

I try to cheer myself up by primping a little, putting on cute clothes and some makeup, but I don't have the heart to brave the flatiron again. I'll stick to my drunken wave.

The party is jumping when we get there, and Sharese and I dance our way inside. Thank God the sound system is playing hip-hop, because I really don't feel like stoner acid jazz. The stoners are around somewhere, though. I can smell them.

We fill plastic cups with beer from the keg and head into the living room. I scan the room for rebound possibilities, even though I realize it's technically impossible to rebound from a relationship that never took place. I wonder if there's such a thing as a crush rebound. I'm thinking like the Oracle again. I've got to stop that.

And then I spot Jared and Brooke.

It didn't even occur to me that they'd be here. How do I take my mind off Jared when he's a few feet away?

"I wish I could run into Mike P. at a party," Sharese says. "Wouldn't that be awesome?"

"Yeah. But there are a lot of other guys here. You shouldn't count them out."

I glance over at Jared. He catches the look and nods, so I nod back and give a polite smile. Brooke sees this, and I can see she's asking, *How do you know her?* He says something back, and suddenly she's waving me over.

I don't exactly like being beckoned, but I have no excuse not to go over there.

I turn to Sharese. "Come with me?"

She shrugs. "Sure."

"Kayla!" To my surprise, Brooke hugs me like she hugs her popular friends. How weird. If she's trying to act like we're friends to impress Jared, she really shouldn't bother. I doubt he cares.

"You guys know Sharese?" I ask.

Jared says, "Hey," and Brooke says, "Of course I know Sharese! We're in math together."

"English," Sharese says behind a tight smile.

Brooke shrugs, flipping her blond hair. "Jared and I were just talking about what an awesome job you did with that speed dating night, Kayla. It'll have to be a tradition from now on." She gives Jared goo-goo eyes. "It's so cool that we met that way."

Jared's eyes flicker left-right-floor. He knows that I know he didn't check her off.

Brooke goes on, "I'm sorry you didn't get to see The Invisible play last week. Jared and the guys were amazing. I can't believe the bouncer treated you that way—talk about humiliating! I don't see why everyone found it so funny."

Jared's eyes zero in on me. "What happened? I didn't know you came to the club."

I avoid looking at him. "I came with my friends. Two

of us got in. I got carded and…the bouncer wasn't impressed with my ID."

"Why didn't you tell me?"

"You can't blame her," Brooke says. "It was brutal. What is it the bouncer said, Kayla? That you look like a freshman? He freaked out on her, threatened to call the police."

She's got this little smirk on her face like she finds this hilarious. I realize this is why she called me over in the first place. To humiliate me.

I should never have gone out tonight. Erland is totally right about Saturn square Jupiter!

Sharese stiffens beside me. "Yeah, well, we had other options that night. I'm glad to see that you and Jared got together, especially after he rejected you at speed dating. A lot of people wouldn't be able to look past that."

Brooke's eyes get so big, her eyelids disappear. *No, you didn't.*

Sharese smiles. *Yes, I did.* She grabs my arm. "Anyway, we'd better get going. Nice meeting you, Jared."

She ushers me into the kitchen and we burst into laughter. Amy and Chad come up, wanting to know what's so funny.

I explain what happened. "Brooke's a bitch," Chad says. "Everyone knows that."

To my surprise, Amy grins. "If she did that, it means one thing—she feels threatened by you." She looks me up and down. "Maybe she saw Jared noticing you. You do look gorgeous tonight."

"For sure," Sharese agrees.

"Thanks, guys." I smile, but I'm still a little traumatized. Jared now knows that I made the effort to show up last Friday night *and* that I brought my friends.

He's probably having a good laugh with Brooke over the whole thing.

THE MORE I THINK ABOUT IT, the more I lose all respect for Jared. Why would he go out with Brooke when he knows she's a fake? His comment on the speed dating card said it all. Doesn't he have any standards?

Or is he, like so many teenage guys, a slave to his hormones?

This is the reason I had my no-dating-until-college rule in the first place. To think I was tempted to break it for Jared!

MONDAY MORNING WHEN HE says hi, I say "hello" in a casual, careless way, then look away. Later in the day, I get to art class early and put my books down on the desk at the back, which is always free. When I spot him coming in, I look down at my sketch, refusing to look at him. I can feel his eyes on me for a few heartbeats as he glances from me to the desk in confusion, but then he goes to the usual desk.

When class starts, I focus on Gerstad, who's talking about painting with watercolors. Out of the corner of my eye, I see Jared glance back a couple of times. At one point my gaze flits over his, and—bam!—our eyes lock. I see his eyes crinkle at the corners with a friendly look, an *innocent* look. What nerve. I roll my eyes, showing him that he just doesn't get it. He frowns and turns back to his work.

Well, one thing's for sure: he knows I'm upset now. And if he's too clueless to figure out why, that's fine with me.

The truth is, I don't really want to punish him. I'm not a vengeful person, really I'm not. I just want to get away from him. Being so near him every day, so near to his cologne and sexy veined forearms, is no way to get over him. It's best if I keep my distance. It would be even better if I didn't have to see him so much, but I'll have to deal with him for the rest of the semester. If I get lucky, we won't have classes together next semester.

Class passes by a lot slower without Jared to chat with. He doesn't glance my way, not even once. I tell myself I'm glad. And yet part of me wants him to come and talk to me, anyway. Part of me wants a Jared fix.

I wonder if this is what drug addiction is like. You want it even though it's killing you. It would be a great concept for a blog, come to think of it: *How Lust is a Drug.* I push the thought aside. There will be no more blogging.

eleven

"Downward facing dog, everyone. Now, hold it in place and breathe. Then slowly raise your head."

I wonder why yoga moves have such strange names. As I raise my head, I wonder why, no matter where I put my yoga mat, my face always ends up mortifyingly close to some woman's spandex-clad butt.

Uh-oh, there it is: the intrusion of thought. Vanessa the instructor says yoga is a form of meditation that should help us distance ourselves from the unhealthy patterns of our thoughts. Which is why I'm taking yoga in the first place. I'm sick of sitting at home ruminating over my mistakes. I've been doing that for two weeks, and it's not working for me. I'm looking for inner peace. Mental stillness. But I can't find it. In fact, whenever I try to still my thoughts, they go out of control and I find myself wondering about odd things, like whether the spandex-clad woman in front of me is wearing underwear.

"Focus on the breath, everyone."

I do. Focus on the breath. Breathe in, breathe out. Do not think of: how I ruined Viv's life, how Jared is a jerk, how I really shouldn't have feelings for him at all, and how feeling depressed is causing me to overeat, making my already tight yoga pants even tighter.

I'm not sure that yoga is for me. It's too introspective. It reminds me how far away I am from zen, nirvana or whatever that blissful state of being is called. It's probably unnatural for someone my age to seek inner peace, anyway; isn't feeling angst a natural part of being a teen?

"Michaela? Do you remember the sun salute?"

Everyone turns to look at me. I hate being singled out. School is bad enough for that, but yoga class? Maybe Vanessa sees me for the fake I am. She knows there's no yogi inside me. Well, it must be easy for *her* to achieve inner peace, being as perfect and blonde as she is. Talk about catty thoughts. Yoga class obviously brings out the worst in me.

When the class is finished, I decide to use the treadmill. I've read that vigorous exercise releases endorphins in the brain and lessens depression, so I might as well give it a go. Unfortunately, I have a strained relationship with treadmills, since I'm always nervous about falling off. Running without going anywhere can't be natural. I start

Allison van Diepen

steadily, gradually ramping it up until my fast walk becomes a slow jog. I feel sweat break out on my forehead, so I must be burning calories. I take it up a notch.

And jog. And jog some more. Damn, this is boring. At least at Tracey's gym, they have TVs in front of you. Here, in place of TVs, the front of the room is lined with mirrors. I have a clear view of the people on the exercise bikes behind me, and the guys pumping iron at the back, sporting wife-beaters and tattoos.

Even though I'm incredibly bored, I'm running at a good pace, and sweating more now. Something in the mirror catches my eye, a familiar figure with red hair. Oh my God, it's Evgeney, and he's doing bicep curls!

My steps falter, and I have to grab the bar to save myself from being swept off the treadmill. I reduce the speed and try to catch my breath. Evgeney works out at the Y? Unbelievable. I never would've pictured it in a million years.

I wonder if…

Of course not. The Oracle never explicitly said a guy should go to the gym. I did say that being strong and masculine was important, though. Is that why he's here?

I should stop thinking about it. I can't attribute Evgeney's fitness routine to the Oracle's advice. He could've been coming here for months, for all I know.

Still, it's cool to see. Maybe I'm not the only one trying to get my life together.

I just hope Evgeney is better at it than I am.

THAT SAME NIGHT, on the other side of town, Tracey is making a very stupid mistake. She stays late at work only to have Scott knocking on her cubicle.

"Hey, Trace."

He's looking überhandsome in a suit he probably can't afford, from what Tracey remembers of his credit card statements. His tie is dangling loose in a rather sexy way. Tracey's always had a weakness for GQ poses, and he knows it.

"Working late again?" Scott asks, leaning on the side of her desk.

Her eyes are focused on the computer screen. "We've got a major project due soon."

"Where are the guys? They all bailed on you?"

"I'm the P.M. for this one. If anyone's going to work late, it should be me."

"P.M., huh? You've moved up in the ranks. I knew Cornheiser would recognize your talent. I'm proud of you, Trace."

"Thanks."

"Have you eaten yet? Let's go to Citarella. I'm in the mood for spicy sausage penne."

Of course, sausage penne is her favorite. And she hasn't eaten since lunch, which makes the thought of food extremely tempting.

Don't go with him! says a voice in the back of her mind. A voice that sounds remarkably like her sister, the Oracle.

It's just dinner, she argues.

It's never just dinner. He's trying to rope you back in. Resist! Resist!

You're right. I know I shouldn't. But I don't care. I'm tired and hungry and I'm sure he's buying.

What? You're going to let yourself be bought?

You know I don't mean it that way. Enough, Kayla!

"Sure, why not? I'm starved."

Tracey tells me all this in an e-mail, not a phone call, obviously because she's afraid to hear my reaction. She didn't go home with him last night, she "got to know him again, as friends" which, to me, is almost as bad. I've only met Scott a few times but his type is universal. He's a *bad* guy (the dreaded opposite of a *good* guy). Tracey doesn't agree because she can see through his cocky exterior to the vulnerable boy beneath. Well, fine, if bad means being a serial killer or a scammer of the elderly then, no, he's not a *bad* guy. But messing with a girl's head and heart makes him a bad boyfriend.

I press Reply.

Dear Trace,

Letting Scott back into your life is a mistake.

I know you're saying you want to be his friend, but you have enough friends already and so does he. If you want a new friend, why make it someone who's already messed you around? Is that a good starting point for a friendship?

Look, I know I often use demonic metaphors when I refer to

him, but I don't really think he's evil. I just think he's screwed up and I'm worried he'll wind up hurting you again.

Trace, I know how much you like to take care of people. But don't worry: if you don't take care of Scott, some other unfortunate soul will!

I believe this friendship thing is Scott's way of regaining your trust. Eventually it will lead to something more, and you'll be in the same situation you were in before. Please don't let that happen. There is a great guy out there for you—I can feel it! You've just got to be patient.

Love, Kayla

Even as I press Send, I know my words won't make any difference. Tracey, a typical Taurus, only listens to what she wants to hear. I can only hope that Tracey makes the right decision in the end. She's older than me, and there's so much more at stake. If she lets Scott in, the worst could happen: they could get married.

But how can she resist temptation when her other recent prospects were a slutty salsa instructor and a guy obsessed with his dog? Compared to them, Scott must look fairly normal.

"I DON'T THINK WE SHOULD go to the dance," I say, making one last attempt at getting out of this. "We should stay home in solidarity with Viv."

My friends roll their eyes. I didn't really expect I could convince them to hang out at Ryan's instead of going to the Halloween dance, but I thought I'd try. I just know it won't be a good time. Saturn is still square Jupiter, so I can't expect anything but lameness (at best) or trouble (at worst).

"Gimme a break," Amy says. "Viv hates dances, anyway. She wouldn't be going even if she weren't grounded."

Good point, I concede silently.

Sharese nods. "And what would we do if we decided not to go—give out candy with Ryan's parents? As if!"

"Fine, I'll go, but...I haven't thought about a costume."

"Of course you haven't," Ryan says with a grin I don't trust. "You never do. That's why we brought some extras for you."

"I'm not going as a prostitute. No way."

Ryan cackles. "Why would you think I'd dress you up as a prostitute? A sexy fairy is far more fun."

I stare at him. "A *sexy* fairy?"

"Yes, a fairy with a little spice. It's an easy costume. Between Amy's pink wig and Sharese's tutu, you'll be fine."

"Did you say tutu?"

Sharese opens a huge garbage bag and pulls out the feathery white tutu. "I haven't worn it for a few years, but it should fit you." She holds it up to my waist.

"I've got the lace cami and nylons." Amy tosses them my way. "It's going to be a fabulous costume. Maybe *I* should've gone with the sexy fairy idea."

Ryan glares at her. "Don't you dare back out of being

Cleopatra. I looked up how to do your makeup and everything."

"I'm not backing out, don't worry. Chad's wearing a toga, too. I wish I had an asp."

"Ta-dah!" Ryan pulls a fake snake out of a drawer. "It's my sister's. I've got an idea. You could slide it down your shirt and have the asp's head peeking out of your cleavage."

"That's awesome!" Amy slides it in, pointing the asp's head to her breast. "Cool! Wait—let's put some makeup on my boob to make it look like I've been bitten. Sharese, where's your red lipstick?"

"Right here, but I've got red lip liner, too—it'll work even better. Who wants to draw it?"

Ryan grabs the lip liner. "I will!"

I shake my head, smiling. My friends get ridiculously excited by Halloween and by school dances—put them together and they go wild. I'm ambivalent about Halloween. I have lots of memories of freezing my butt off trick-or-treating, and going to school in cheesy, thrown-together costumes. School dances are usually okay, but I've never enjoyed the standing-by-the-wall part when slow dances come on. I mean, I can only dance with Ryan so many times, and he has to make the rounds among all of us. Why can't the DJs do what they do at most clubs and keep the music upbeat the whole time? If people want to dance together, they'll dance to fast songs.

By the time my friends are done with me, I have to

admit, they've done a good job. Between the poofy tutu and lacy cami, I've got a cute, sexy getup, though it shows off more of my legs than I'd normally show. Good thing Mom and Erland won't be seeing me before I go. As for the wig, it's a glossy ice-pink bob and it sets off the costume. My makeup is pale and powdery except for false eyelashes and shiny pink lips. For shoes, I'm wearing Sharese's old ballet slippers, which are a size too big, but I'll manage.

Amy and Ryan look awesome as Cleopatra and Julius Caesar (Chad will join them as Mark Antony), and Sharese is in head-to-toe red as a little devil, complete with horns, tail and pitchfork.

We're ready way too early, so we pump up the music in Ryan's bedroom and snap some pictures. Chad picks us up at eight-thirty and we pile into the car, a tangled mess of wings and horns and wreaths. When we arrive at the dance, the parking lot is almost full, but Chad kindly drops us off at the door before going to park.

Thank God I brought a coat, because we have to wait outside for fifteen minutes before we get in, and my legs are freezing under the tutu, my knees knocking together like chattering teeth. Female security guards give us a pat down and check our bags—as if we'd be stupid enough to smuggle booze into a dance. Anyone who wants to drink does it before the dance, not during.

Once we get through Security, we check our coats and

head into the hot, crowded gym, sliding into the mix of dancers alongside some people we know. As I start dancing, I immediately spot Jared and Brooke, and wish I hadn't. Brooke is Miss New York, her hair twirled on top of her head, a sparkling blue dress hugging her curves and a Miss New York sash over her shoulder, not to mention a tiara. Jared's wearing an old-fashioned suit and top hat. Half of his face is covered in a gross, mottled mask. Jekyll and Hyde. How fitting.

Jared tears off his mask, accidentally knocking off his top hat. He picks it up, then rakes a hand through his hair, scowling. I can see in that scowl that he's hot, annoyed and feeling like a dork. I can't help but laugh.

Which, of course, is when he sees me. His eyes widen as if he can't believe it's me. I know I look silly, but he doesn't need to stare like that. A group of people block our vision, which is just as well.

The next song is upbeat, and the dancers pick up the pace. Suddenly people are moving back and creating a circle. No way I'm getting in the middle. I see Brooke and her friends, Miss New Jersey, Miss California and Miss Hawaii, strut into the middle and start dancing with one another sensually, trying to turn on all the guys. I glimpse Jared, who doesn't look impressed. It's not that he looks angry, exactly. He just looks bored.

Sharese grabs my arm, turning my attention back to the circle. Evgeney has joined the girls in the middle, thrusting himself into the melee. He's dressed as a werewolf in heavy fur from head to toe, but his head and face are uncovered, his red hair spiked with sweat or gel. The girls don't seem to know how to deal with this sudden invasion, so they just go with it. And Evgeney is taking full advantage, bucking against them like a horny bull.

Sharese claps and hoots. "That guy's got balls!"

He sure does. Evgeney goes from dancing with the girls to taking over the show, calling upon a treasure trove of dance moves the likes of which I've never seen. He's pushing his arms out in front of him as if he's doing push-ups, while his legs are doing some sort of grapevine, or country music line dance. Then his arms are swinging in front of him like he's erasing a chalkboard with both hands, then they're flailing from side to side as if he's grabbing groceries off shelves and dropping them into a shopping cart, then he's leaping all over the place like a gazelle in Madame Butterfly. It's pure awesomeness, and we're all crying with laughter. Evgeney looks around and grins. I guess that was his intention, to entertain us. Then he leaps back into the crowd, and the circles closes.

"Evgeney rocks!" Ryan shouts. "He stole their thunder!" We all agree, wiping our tears.

The song changes, and we're bouncing to some hip-hop. I spot Declan McCall and his football buddies jumping around like crazy people. At least Evgeney *meant* to be entertaining—I think Declan and his friends are just overenthusiastic. I realize it's a double standard; girls can bop all over the dance floor and be called cute, but guys, on the other hand, should keep the bopping under control if they're not to endanger their masculinity. I mean, some guys—like Chad—can dance naturally without looking like an idiot. Ryan can, too. But Declan McCall and his friends obviously can't. They're hopping around like Mexican jumping beans and thrusting out their arms as if they're boxing with imaginary opponents. Weird.

When the flow of the dance floor brings our group closer to theirs, I can smell the alcohol on them. I wonder how they got in reeking like that, or whether they managed to smuggle it in. I wish I could write a blog for Declan and his friends about how not to look dumb at a school dance. I'm all for people expressing themselves through dance, but this is ridiculous. And then an elbow hits my ribs.

"Ow!"

"Sorry, Kayla," Declan says, breathing booze in my direction.

He knows my name? Well, I guess I shouldn't be surprised; we've spent the past ten years or so going to school together. But I've never been a part of the cult of personality that has surrounded Declan; he was always a golden boy, ever since he was a kid, and I'm not into golden boys. I'm into… I will so not look over at Jared.

I feel hands grab my hips, and I realize that Declan is dancing with me. Judging by the looks on my friends' faces, I've scored. Scored *what* I don't know, but who cares? No

one needs to know that Declan is too drunk to find someone else or that I can smell his beer breath. It doesn't smell
bad, actually, mixed with his minty mouthwash.

I turn around, and we're dancing together. He's got a
goofy smile on his face like he's enjoying himself, and I
can't help smiling, too. I'm aware of the fact that this could
boost my reputation, albeit temporarily. And why not get
some tongues wagging? I've had such a crappy couple of
weeks, I could use some good press.

Speaking of tongues wagging, Declan's face is hovering
a little too close to mine. His lips swoop down, but only
catch my cheek. *What is he doing?* I'm not going to make
out with a guy I'm not even dating. I mean, I might do
that *elsewhere,* like at a bar, but not at a school dance. If I
make out with him, I'd look stupid next week when he
ignores me. I wouldn't let just anyone kiss me. Even
Melvin, my birthday kiss, had some redeeming qualities.

The song changes again, but he doesn't release me from
his grip, so I settle in, comfortably dancing in the cocoon
of his arms. He seems to be having fun playing with my
tutu, which makes me laugh. Nearby—nearer than they
were a couple of minutes ago—Jared and Brooke and their
friends are dancing. For a second, I catch Jared's eye, and he
stares at me intently, as if he's trying to send me a message.
But I don't know what he's getting at, so I shrug it off.

I have to say, Jared looks like a fish out of water. Brooke
and Kirsten Cook are gyrating on either side of him,

creating a Jared sandwich. He's frowning as if he never intended to be part of such a sandwich.

When the music changes to a boppy song, I glance at Jared, who looks like he wants to shoot himself. I see him try to leave the dance floor, but Brooke grabs his arm. He shakes her off and walks away. Brooke glances at Declan, as if to see if he noticed the exchange, but Declan is still focused on playing with my tutu. She looks even angrier and stalks off the dance floor.

Soon after, a slow song comes on. To my surprise, Declan doesn't move along to another girl, he hugs me close. I have to admit, it feels good having his strong body against me, even if he's on the sweaty side. There's something about being close to a guy, even if it doesn't mean anything. I think about Tracey, and send up a prayer that she's not with Scott right now.

Declan tries to kiss me again, and I only narrowly dodge it. "Hey, don't get fresh," I tell him, hoping he'll get the picture. A couple of minutes later, his hands slip to my butt, and I take a step back, saying, "I don't think so." He grins sheepishly and moves his hands back to my waist.

As the ballad fades, I feel a hand on my shoulder, and turn to find myself staring into Jared's cool blue eyes. "You promised me a slow dance. It's our last chance."

"Um, okay." I turn to Declan.

He looks mildly annoyed, but also tired and drunk. "I'll get a drink," he says. "You want a drink, Kayla?"

"No, thanks."

Declan moves away. All around us, couples are changing partners, leaving or coming onto the dance floor. Jared puts his arms around me rather stiffly.

"What's going on?" I shout over the music.

"You and Declan. He's bad news."

"What do you mean?"

"He treated Brooke like shit. Totally screwed her up."

"We were just dancing. It wasn't going to go any further than that."

"I hear he's a charmer."

I have to laugh. "Who says? Charming guys don't smell like beer and try to grope your butt."

Jared looks disgusted. "Then why'd you bother with him?"

"I don't know. It was just something to do. Where's Brooke, anyway?"

"She left. I'm meeting her later."

"Whatever." It came out snarky, but I can't take it back. I notice the way he's holding me at arm's length; we look like grade sevens who can't stand touching the opposite sex. I step back.

"Look, you wanted to say your piece about Declan, and you did. Thanks. Now I'm going to get something to eat."

His eyes flicker. "I'd better go."

And we leave the dance floor, forking off in different directions.

twelve

I WISH HE HADN'T DONE THAT, I tell myself for the hundredth time. As I'm lying in bed later that night, I can't get Jared out of my mind. Why did he care if I was dancing with Declan or not? He must care about me, even if it's just as a friend. Of course it's just as a friend, I remind myself—he's dating Brooke, not me.

What he did was gallant, even though it was totally unnecessary. It's not like Declan or I had any real intentions. In fact, Declan never came back to me. Instead he moved on to a freshman who had no hesitations about getting some tongue action. I doubt he'll remember our little dance, and it's just as well.

It was strange, though, the way Jared held me. It was like he felt awkward about getting physically close to me. But why? Oh, I've got it. Even though Brooke had already gone, some of her friends were still there. If Jared was seen

Allison van Diepen

to be getting close to another girl, it would get back to Brooke, and she would freak.

Picturing Jared as a whipped boyfriend is hard to do, but I can't think of any other explanation. He was definitely keeping my body at a distance. I'd love to think it's because my nearness drove him wild, but maybe he just didn't want to tangle with my tutu.

I can't believe I'm pining for a guy with a girlfriend. If someone had called the Oracle with this problem, I would've told her to move on.

But what if they'd told me the guy had cut in while she was dancing with another guy and seemed concerned about her welfare? What would the Oracle say then?

SUNDAY NIGHT AT AMY'S, my friends hurl questions at me left and right. What was it like dancing with Declan? What sweet nothings did he whisper in my ear? Why did Jared cut in, and why did he look angry? Why didn't I slip my phone number in Declan's pocket so he'd find it when he sobered up?

I don't give them any juicy tidbits to satisfy them. If they knew he tried to kiss me and grope me, they'd blow it out of proportion and I'd never live it down. So I tell them that I met Declan's criteria for a dance partner (female), and that Jared wasn't some jealous lover, but rather a concerned friend who wanted to warn me against getting involved with Declan. Yada yada yada.

When I get home, I'm not in my bedroom five minutes when Viv IMs me wanting to hear about the dance. Thankfully, I manage to steer the conversation to Evgeney's wild performance.

LostGirl: For the first time, I'm sorry I missed a school dance. Seeing Evgeney dance like a maniac sounds like a once-in-a-lifetime experience.

Kaylalala: Judging by the way he was received, he'll be doing it again. Maybe dressed as an elf at the Christmas dance. You'll have to come just in case.

LostGirl: I will. *sigh* My grounding will be over by then, thank God. I haven't been out in ages.

Kaylalala: We'll have to go out and celebrate afterward. How are you feeling? I mean, about the Max thing…

LostGirl: I'm doing okay. I think Max and I are going to be friends again. We've texted a bit in the past few days.

Kaylalala: Is he handling it better?

LostGirl: Yeah. He still thinks we'll get together one day… For now, we're not ready to sever the friendship.

Kayalalala: Less than two years until you're off to college. Then you'll do what you want.

LostGirl: Exactly. My parents know that they can only control me while I'm under their roof. After that, they're going to have to accept my decisions. I don't

know what the future holds for me and Max. But for now,
at least we can be friends.

Kaylalala: I'm so glad.

LostGirl: When are you going to put the Oracle site back
up? I need more of your blogs to read.

**Kaylalala: Not this again. I told you, the Oracle isn't
coming back.**

LostGirl: But there's nothing like it out there! Most
advice sites are run by adults and are totally lame.
You've got to put it back up!

Kaylalala: I'm sorry, Viv. I can't.

LostGirl: You're so stubborn! The world *needs* the Oracle.

Kaylalala: Look, it's late. We'd better get to bed.

LostGirl: Fine. Just promise me you'll think about it.

Kaylalala: I'll think about it.

But I knew I wouldn't be putting the site back up. The
Oracle is dead and gone.

MONDAY MORNING, the hallways are buzzing with gossip.

Amy is ready with the scoop when I get to my locker.
"You'll never believe it—Brooke dumped Jared! They had
this huge fight after the dance Friday night. Apparently
he wanted to have sex and she didn't. We all know Declan
was her first. I guess she wasn't ready for another one yet."

"*What?* Who said this?"

"Brooke. She's telling everyone he's an asshole—which I guess he is. I mean, come on, what kind of guy can't wait more than two weeks for sex?"

What kind of guy indeed? I wonder if there's more to the story.

"What does Jared say about this?"

"When Andrew Becker asked him, he pretty much confirmed it."

"Pretty much?"

"He didn't *deny* it."

"So he neither confirmed nor denied it."

"Something like that. Brooke won't let her friends talk to him anymore, so he's back to being an outsider. That's the shortest time at the top I've ever seen!"

My first thought: Poor Jared. My second thought: Wait a minute—if Brooke's story is true, he got what he deserved!

When I walk into class, Jared is at his desk, doodling as usual. He looks up and says hi, smiling at me. It's a cheerful smile, which catches me off guard. We're not in the habit of exchanging smiles like that anymore. And shouldn't he be depressed about the breakup?

Apparently not, because his mood is so good, he's humming a tune.

I am dying to know what really happened. I mean, the Oracle side of me is dying to know. Isn't a match between a hottie and a hot rocker made in heaven?

But I don't have the guts to ask Jared if the rumors are true. It's none of my business, anyway.

We don't interact for the rest of the class. At lunchtime, as I'm eating fish sticks and tartar sauce, I keep thinking: a) Jared can't possibly be as bad as Brooke is portraying him. b) Jared could be as bad as Brooke is portraying him. c) I'm almost over him. Almost. So Jared being single should mean nothing to me. d) If b) is true, then I wouldn't want to be with Jared, anyway. e) This cafeteria food is terrible. I have to start packing a lunch.

"I know what you mean," Viv says. "I don't think it's really tartar sauce—it's just mayo."

I look up. Did I say it aloud? I hope I didn't say *all* of my thoughts aloud.

Sharese slides in beside us with her lunch tray. "Hey, guys. Did you hear about Jared and Brooke?"

Ryan nods. "Shocking, huh? Who knew Brooke would refuse to give it up?"

"That's not the shocking part," Sharese says. "It's that Jared was such a jerk. And I thought he was a nice guy for warning Kayla against Declan."

"You can't believe everything you hear," Viv points out. "We're just hearing Brooke's version."

"Yeah, but Mark Baker—you know, from the Environment Club—went up to Jared and asked him if it was true, and Jared said yes!"

That's damning information. Everyone knows Mark Baker is the school's ethicist and moral puritan. He wouldn't lie about what Jared said.

So it really is true.

I feel something inside me sink. Sure, I'd already decided that Jared was an idiot for going out with Brooke, but I guess I'd been hoping he'd redeem himself. If Jared actually treated Brooke that way, then he really is a jerk. And I'm lucky I never got involved with him.

It's strange, though. Why didn't he deny the story? Then it would be his word against Brooke's, and since she's known for being a drama queen, a lot of people would doubt her story. Why did he confirm it?

As the day wears on, I'm no closer to understanding the situation. My intuition tells me that Jared would never be aggressive that way. Or are my feelings for him clouding my judgment?

In art class, I can't take my eyes off him. Thankfully, he doesn't know I'm staring, because he's two tables in front of me. Weird, but I really thought I had good instincts about people. Like with Scott, for instance. I pegged him for an emotional pariah the moment I set eyes on him. I knew he'd hurt my sister, and he did.

But Jared was different. Despite having a certain arrogance and antisocial bent, despite the mistakes of his past,

I thought he was, deep down, a good person. Maybe at some level I told myself that Brooke had brainwashed him into going out with her, and that he'd smarten up soon enough.

Jared turns his head, his eyes questioning. I feel heat rush into my cheeks. He must've felt me staring at him. He raises his eyebrows and beckons me. I look around in confusion, realizing that people are pairing up.

Uh-oh. I have to work with him again. Maybe I should try to find another partner. But it's too late—Jared's taken my hesitation for a yes. He picks up his stuff and puts it down beside me.

"I didn't catch the instructions," I say.

"We're drawing hands."

I give him a blank look.

"I'll show you. Cup your hands and rest them on the desk. I'll draw them."

Another impossible assignment. I cup my hands and put them on the desk. He stares at them and begins to draw.

The silence between us is painful. Occasionally he'll ask me to move my hands this way or that, but he never touches them. I feel like I should say something, but I don't know what.

"Did the dance get any better after I left?"

"They didn't play Vengeance Against the Establishment, if that's what you mean."

"So you had fun?"

"Yeah. It'll go down in history as the best dance ever."

"Why's that?"

"Because of Evgeney Vraslov's dance show."

He quirks a smile, though his eyes are still fixated on my hands. "I saw that."

"Sorry to hear about…you know."

He raises his head. "About what?"

He appears genuine, but I figure he's not making this easy for me. "You know, you and Brooke breaking up."

A wicked look enters his eyes. "Are you *really* sorry?"

I swallow. What's he getting at?

"C'mon, Kayla. You're no fan of Brooke. Truth is, I don't think I ever was, either. So there's no need to be sorry."

He continues drawing in silence. When he's done, the resulting sketch is wonderful, as usual. He makes my hands look far more elegant than they really are. Now I have to draw his hands. Oh, joy. He places his hands on the desk, cupping them together. And for a second I think about what it would be like for one of his big, strong hands to hold mine. And then I picture those hands groping Brooke.

Jared looks at me. "Something wrong?"

"No. I'm just frustrated—you know I can't draw."

"Your other project's coming along nicely."

"I still have to paint it. I could ruin everything."

His eyes narrow. "What's up with you these days, Kayla? You're on edge or something."

"What are you talking about?"

"You. How you've been lately. You go switching desks and you don't even say why. And you're not…cheerful anymore."

"Was I ever cheerful?"

"Actually, yeah. Now it's like you've got PMS every day."

My jaw must've hit the floor. "Thanks *a lot*. Let's just get this done, okay? I need this grade." I'm sketching again and making a mess of things.

He touches my hand. "Sorry. I thought you'd laugh. We always give each other a hard time, don't we?"

I glance at him. "Yeah."

"So I guess you heard the story of what happened between Brooke and me."

"I heard."

"And? What do you think?"

"I think there's more to the story. There always is. And I think part of this is your fault for not denying it when you had the chance."

"Why should I? No one cares about the truth."

"So are you saying it's not the truth?"

His eyes lock with mine, like he's seeing right through me. "Do you care about the truth?"

"Yes."

"Fine. Ask yourself this—what if the person you're dating is a total pain in the ass, and the only thing that remotely interests you is the possibility of having sex?"

"Are you serious?"

"Partly."

"So it *is* true."

"Look, Brooke and I weren't good together, anyway. She's totally self-centered and jealous. That's why she embarrassed you at the party. I'm glad your friend put her in her place. I wish I'd been quick enough to do it myself. Brooke was going on about it the rest of the night. She's in love with drama. Anyway, she was never interested in the real me. She just wanted to date a musician."

"But you still wanted to have sex with her?"

"I wanted to scare her off. So I told her it was time we had sex, and I wasn't all that nice about it."

"Wait, back up a minute. You said that to make her dump you?"

"Yeah. She'd already told me she wasn't ready, so I figured it was a safe bet. I didn't think she could take another rejection."

"But you're hurting your own reputation! You must've known she'd go around telling everyone."

"Of course I did. How does that hurt my reputation? I'm just another guy who wants sex. So what? At least this way Brooke can hate me instead of getting all broken up about it."

"I still don't get it. If she was so annoying, why do you care so much about her ego?"

"She's still upset over Declan dumping her. He treated her like shit. Anyway, she's gotta be the most insecure person I've ever met. I didn't want to see her get hurt again."

"I can't believe this. You did that out of *compassion*. And now everyone who likes her is ostracizing you."

He winks. "That's just a bonus."

thirteen

"Jay, CAN YOU OPEN your cash, please?" I say into the intercom. "Jay, open your cash!"

I have a dozen angry customers in my line, and my pothead coworker is nowhere to be found. I might as well have stayed home and self-flagellated like the albino in *The Da Vinci Code*.

Spotting a familiar face in line, I smile and wave. Lucy Ball is huddled over her shopping cart. The sight of her lightens my mood. She doesn't mind a line, not like other people do. When she gets to the front of the line, she says, "How are you, Michaela?"

"Pretty good, Short Stuff. What about yourself?"

"I can't complain. How is your advice business going?"

Incredible how she remembers everything I tell her. "Actually, I've decided to close up shop."

"That's too bad. You seemed so excited about it."

"It's not a big deal." I shrug and continue scanning her groceries. "I should be saving up for college, anyway, and this job helps."

She leans closer and whispers, "Smart girl like you can find a better job than this."

I smile, because Lucy Ball gets it. I should really start looking for another job. When you're unhappy doing what you're doing, you've got to make a change. I only wish I knew what that change was. A new job won't change the fact that I'm not the Oracle anymore.

After my lineup thins, the night drags by at a snail's pace. I get home from work at nine-forty-five, depleted. All I want is a bowl of comfort cereal, my bed and the abyss of sleep.

As soon as I'm in my bedroom, I go to the computer and check my e-mail. Nothing. I haven't heard from Tracey in days and it worries me. My intuition is telling me it has something to do with Scott. I hope my intuition fails me this once!

I log into Facebook and see that Viv has put a couple of comments on my profile. It looks like she was bored and looking to chat.

Seeing that I have a new group invitation, I click on it. The group is called *Bring Back the Oracle of Dating!*

No. Way.

At the top it says, *This group is for people who think the Oracle of Dating is fantastic. We stand united in wanting her to put her Web site back up!* The moderator is Viv. And there are seventy-four members.

Seventy-four members—holy crap! That's a lot, especially since the group only started three days ago.

But I'm sure it's just Viv trying to make me feel better. These members probably aren't even interested in the Oracle. I know that because I join most groups I'm invited to.

I scroll down to the message board.

"The Oracle helped me realize I needed to love myself before I could love someone else," a girl named Katrina writes.

"I never paid for advice from the Oracle, but her blog is awesome. She really tells it like it is!" says a kid named Jamie.

"Viv, why are you so obsessed with the Oracle of Dating?" Amy writes. *"Okay, I admit, that blog on make-out buddies was interesting."*

"The Oracle tries her best to give advice even when the situation is complicated," Viv writes. *"I give her a lot of credit for that."*

There are a few other testimonials and a discussion about why the Oracle Web site was taken down. Some people speculate that the Oracle wasn't making enough money to keep the site and phone line running. One person suggests it's because the Oracle's in high school and has exams coming up. Others say that she made so much money she didn't need to do it anymore. Now, *that's* funny.

"I'm sure the Oracle never got rich," Viv wrote. *"She obviously did it because she wanted to help people. You can tell it's a calling for her."*

As I'm reading the discussions, another comment pops up on the page. It's from Evgeney. His profile picture is a shot of him staring intently into his Web cam as if he's trying to figure out if it's broken. *"The Oracle of Dating is excellent. The advice is very wise. It is not just for women. She gives advice to men, too. We need the Oracle to come back!"*

Tears prick at my eyes. Evgeney *was* reading the site, just like I'd hoped. That must be why he started working out. I wipe my tears. Ridiculous to cry like this. But it's such a relief to know that I actually helped people instead of just screwing up their lives.

I have to wonder: am I letting people like Evgeney down just because I'm afraid of giving bad advice again?

Maybe the risk of giving bad advice is part of the deal. If I'm going to help people, I have to accept that sometimes I'll make a mistake. But it's worth it if I can help most people, isn't it?

I shouldn't quit because of my failure with Viv. And she's known that all along.

With shaky fingers, I write her an e-mail. "Thank you, Viv. You can announce on the Facebook group that the Oracle plans to put the Web site back up again tomorrow at 4:00 p.m. EST. And please tell them that I'm thankful for all of their encouragement."

I send the e-mail, a feeling of peace coming over me. Idly I scroll through the group's members. I blink when I spot the profile of Jared Stewart, whose picture is a vintage electric guitar. What's he doing on a group supporting the Oracle? I didn't even know he was on Facebook.

I feel myself smile. If the Oracle can get the attention of a skeptic like Jared, I must've been doing something right.

THE NEXT DAY AT SCHOOL, I'm different. I'm walking with a smile on my face and a spring in my step. I can't wait to rush home later today and upload the source files, watch the screen light up in pink and blue.

In class, Jared catches my eye. "You're in a good mood today." There's a teasing light in his eyes.

"You're right."

"So what's got you happy?"

I can't exactly elaborate and tell him why. "Just… stuff." And, thankfully, that's when Ms. Goff starts the lesson.

At lunchtime in the caf, Viv exchanges a grin with me. I bet she's already announced on the Facebook group that the Oracle will be up and running today after school. It's good to see her smiling. I'm smiling, too.

"The Oracle of Dating e-mailed me last night to say that she's putting the Web site up again," Viv announces.

Ryan raises his brows. "Wow—your group really worked!"

"I'm not sure my group's what did it. I think the Oracle knew she had no choice but to come back. She can't turn away people in need."

"You're too modest," Sharese says. "I bet your group

helped. So, if the Oracle e-mailed you, does that mean you know who it is? I guess not some old businessman like I thought?"

Viv smiles. "She's just a girl like us who's into giving advice."

"Well, if she can help Evgeney, she deserves a medal," Sharese says. "Did you see what he posted on Facebook last night?"

We all nod.

Ryan scratches his head. "He must've been a big fan of the Oracle. I wonder if he read something on the site that made him change the way he dressed."

"I'm sure he did," Viv tells him.

"Evgeney's dressing differently?" I hadn't seen him lately, except that time at the gym and at the dance. We don't have any classes together.

"Really," Ryan says. "No more big collars. And I'm pretty sure he attempted to gel his hair the other day."

I can't help but smile. "Good for him. He's such a nice guy."

"Yeah, well. You know what they say about nice guys," Sharese says dismally.

"What's wrong with nice guys?" Viv asks.

"They finish last."

Viv shakes her head. "That's just a cliché."

"They certainly finish last in the money department," Ryan says. "You don't make money by being nice."

"But a nice guy will always find a nice girl," I say.

"I bet you're waiting for a nice guy to find you, huh, Kayla?" Sharese asks.

I shrug. "Maybe."

"Well, I think Evgeney will find a nice girl sooner or later with the help of the Oracle." Viv is careful not to look at me. "With Evgeney, she's got her work cut out for her."

THAT NIGHT, I'M SWAMPED with calls, instant messages and e-mails. I pass on having coffee with Amy and Sharese so that I can attend to my clients. Thank God I don't have a shift at Eddie's.

I post a message on the home page: "Due to personal reasons, the Oracle of Dating Web site has been down recently, but now it is back up. The Oracle apologizes for any difficulty this has caused, and assures you that she is here to stay!"

I get so many e-mails that I have to remind myself to go slow, and to consult sources where needed. When I get a couple of particularly difficult questions, I e-mail the clients back saying that the Oracle will need a couple of days to "meditate" on them. I refuse to give an off-the-cuff answer like the one I gave to Viv.

One female e-mailer even asks me for fashion advice. She must have concluded that, since I'd given some guys' clothing advice in a blog meant for Evgeney, fashion was part of my area of expertise. Hmm. Maybe it could be. I'll have to quiz Ryan on the season's trends.

Around nine I hurry downstairs to grab my nightly bowl of cereal. Before I can run back upstairs, Erland shouts, "The Saturn-Jupiter aspect is over now!"

"Thanks, Erland!" I could've told him that.

THE NEXT WEEK GOES BY in a haze of school, dating questions, blogging and all things Oracle. Even while I'm working at the Hellhole, I find myself making notes on dating issues when I have a spare minute. It's as if the weeks of not being the Oracle caused all this creativity to be suppressed, and now it's coming out in a flood.

I meet with Erland to get astrological predictions for the coming week, telling him that I'd like to do love horoscopes for all my friends (which isn't a lie, not really). I make notes as he describes the traits of different astrological signs, and explains what the current transits might mean for them next week.

While it's all fresh in my mind, I hurry upstairs to write up the love horoscopes. It's a lot of fun to do, and I have the satisfaction of knowing they're based on real astrology. Once I've finished writing all twelve, I take a closer look at my own.

Libra: The sign for Libra is the scales of justice, which means that you're mostly concerned with the well-being of others. Unfortunately, that also means that you usually put the interests of others above your own. This week, that has to change. The Oracle would like you to pay some attention to your *life—specifically,* your *love life. By taking care of your needs, you will be all the better prepared to help others.*

It totally rings true. These days I've been so into being the Oracle again that I've been neglecting the open window in my love life. Jared is single again; isn't it a chance I would've died for a few weeks ago? What more do I need?

But it's not as easy as just asking him out, I know that. I've got to do it in a more subtle way. Who can help me but the Oracle?

Glancing back through the Web site archives, I find a blog aptly called:

How to Make Him Ask You Out

1. Smile at him A LOT. Be warm and open. Flirt with him (if you've forgotten how, see my blog on flirting).

2. Give him an opening—for example, mention you haven't figured out your Saturday-night plans yet.

3. Ask what he did on the weekend—that will let him know you're interested in what he's up to outside of school or work.

4. Suggest a casual group get-together. It could help break the ice. You could say, "My friends are going downtown tonight. We should all meet up and play pool."

Allison van Diepen

```
5. Feel free to e-mail or call him on an unrelated
issue—it may pave the way for him to ask you out.

6. Ask him out yourself. Too shy? Do everything else on
this list.
```

I take a deep breath. The advice isn't bad, if I do say so myself.

Unless Jared is totally blind, he can see that I like him. I'm letting him know in every way besides actually telling him. I'm smiling, joking around. And he knows that I tried to go to his show. Shouldn't that mean something?

Gossip about Jared has died down lately, especially since Brooke is now directing her attention toward winning back Declan. Jared is again on the periphery, and he doesn't seem to mind. It's the time of year when most mammals choose their winter hibernation partner and get ready for the season of snuggling. We've got downright warmth flowing between us. So what about the next step? Why are we both afraid to take the plunge?

Or am I completely and utterly delusional to think Jared has any interest in me, like so many of those unfortunate speed daters?

This is getting ridiculous. I have to do something. There's not much time. Who knows what other girl might get in the way?

When I walk into the art room the next day, I find Jared

already hard at work. I put my books down beside him. "Working on your project?"

"No, I'm already done. I'm working on something else."

"Can I see?"

"All right." He moves his arm out of the way.

He's done a beautiful drawing of the Afghan girl from the magazine cover. He's captured the girl so perfectly, it could almost be mistaken for the photo itself.

"You like it?"

"It's mind-blowing."

"Thanks. I'll let you hand it in for, say, fifty bucks?"

I see the glint in his eye and smack him on the arm. "Don't tempt me. Not that anyone would believe I did this. Why aren't you handing it in yourself?"

"I need it for my portfolio. I'm applying to art school."

"Art school? Wow."

"What's so surprising about that?"

"Nothing. It's just not the usual path. It's cool."

"What about you? I bet you've got a plan of some kind. Let me guess—you're going to be an entrepreneur and start a dating service."

I stare at him. He can't know, can he? "Why would you say that?"

"You organized the speed dating night. Maybe you caught the matchmaking bug."

"Oh, right. I was thinking more of being a relationship counselor."

"I could see you being a counselor. You've got the friendly thing going on. I mean, when you don't have PMS."

"I can't believe you just said that."

"Well, I did." He moves close to me, so that his chest is inches from mine. "What are you gonna do? Kick my ass?"

We stare into each other's eyes for one intense moment, and suddenly we're laughing.

Gerstad shushes us. We stop laughing, but every time we look at each other we want to burst out all over again.

As class ends, he slips me a note.

You're crazy, Kayla. But you make me laugh. Let's meet for coffee tonight.

Oh. My. God. He has no idea how long I've been waiting for this!

Sure. Call me after school. 555-3940.

He nods. He's looking, suddenly, a little shy. Like I'm feeling.

I guess we both know…

It's a date.

Wohoooo!!!! Sorry. I just had to get that out.

fourteen

JARED SUGGESTS WE MEET at the Tea Lounge in Park Slope at eight.

What should I wear? The Oracle would caution that if I dress up too much, or put on more makeup than usual, Jared will sense that I'm really, eagerly into him. So cute-casual is the look I'm going for. I put on my Gap jeans and a black velvet hoodie, and wear the same sneakers I wore at school. My hair stays loose around my shoulders, drunken wave and all. I redo my eyeliner and lip gloss but leave it at that.

"Where are you going, honey?" Mom asks as I'm heading toward the door. She and the Swede are in the living room, drinking tea and watching the news.

"I have a date. I won't be out late."

Mom looks surprised. The Swede doesn't, and I notice a slight smile. I don't wait for questions, I grab my jacket and head out the door.

The Tea Lounge is a cozy place on Union Street across from a natural-food co-op. It's only two stops away, and I end up arriving fifteen minutes early. I might as well take a seat and wait inside, because it's cold and I don't want to be all red-nosed and shivery when I see him.

When I walk in, my gaze sweeps the place for free seats and I spot Jared sitting on the couch chatting with some big muscular guy with long dark hair. I take in the sight of Jared, feeling my knees weaken, thinking how he makes all other guys my age look boring. Then I notice he's wearing the same clothes he wore to school and it hits me that I shouldn't have changed—damn!

The big guy next to him has a notepad on his lap and they seem to be talking intently. I wonder if he's Jared's band's manager.

Jared looks up and waves. I approach. "Sorry I'm early. I don't want to interrupt."

"Who cares? This is my social worker, Rodrigo. This is Kayla, my fellow artist."

Rodrigo smiles and shakes my hand. "Great to meet you, Kayla."

"Nice to meet you, too."

Rodrigo hoists his leather bag over his shoulder. "Well, I'll leave you to it. See you next time, Jared." As Rodrigo walks away, it hits me. Though I'm not prone to psychic instincts, something about that guy, that gentle giant, makes me think he'd be perfect for Tracey.

"Tell me more about Rodrigo. Is he single?"

Jared stares at me. "You're kidding me, right? The guy's, like, thirty."

"So? There are still some single guys who are thirty, aren't there?"

Jared's mouth moves like he's trying to find words. "Uh, yeah, he's single."

"Perfect! Wait, do you mean single as in he's not married? He doesn't have a girlfriend, does he?"

"Not that I know of."

"Do you think he'd be willing to be set up? I think he'd love my sister. She's really the sweetest—"

Jared's laugh cuts me off. "Your sister? God, I thought you were talking about yourself."

"Myself? Yeah, right. He's way too old for me."

"You're right. He is. Now, let's get drinks, okay?"

As we head to the bar, I catch a whiff of his cologne. If my nostrils are correct, it's something different from what he was wearing earlier. Ha! A sign of effort!

I can't believe we're actually *on a date*. Joy rushes through me, followed by trepidation. Maybe I shouldn't have started out by questioning him about Rodrigo's romantic status. It didn't occur to me that Jared would think I was asking for myself. I mean, for a sixteen-year-old to go after a guy who's clearly thirty is ridiculous, though I know it happens. I'll hold off on quizzing him about Rodrigo's relationship history for now, and focus on creating one with me and Jared.

Allison van Diepen

We buy some drinks—blueberry soy smoothie for me, caramel latte for him—and go back to sit on the couch. The first couple of minutes are a little, er, um, awkward. It's as if we've both realized that this isn't art class, and we aren't sure how to act. Plus I'm having a thousand mini panic attacks (*I'm on a date with Jared! This is unreal!*), and I have to force myself to focus on what he's saying. Once I do, the conversation flows better and the tension eases.

"So tell me about this art school you're applying to," I say, stirring the thick smoothie, trying to still my mind like in yoga class, trying *not* to wonder if he's going to kiss me right here on the couch, or on a windy street corner, either of which would be fine with me.

"I want to do Fine Arts at City College. That's actually what Rodrigo and I were talking about. He's helping me look into scholarships. I'm working as much as I can to save the tuition."

"Where do you work?"

"I teach art classes to kids at the youth center. It's an after-school program, so it doesn't pay much. The rest of the time I pump gas at Cecil's on Nostrand."

"I work at Eddie's Grocery. We're not even allowed to have a cup for tips. Not that people would tip us, anyway. It's a horrible store."

"That sucks. I don't know about you, but I've been working crappy jobs for years."

"I shouldn't complain. I only started at Eddie's last year."

"You live with your parents, right?"

"My mom and stepdad. My dad lives in Canada."

"Your mom and stepdad get along okay?"

"Yeah. They sit around for hours reading and drinking tea. Sometimes they talk philosophy and theology. It's like PBS's idea of a sitcom. Anyway, Mom's happy, which is the most important thing."

"What about you? You like your stepdad?"

To my surprise, I hesitate before answering. "Not long ago, I might've said I was neutral. But he's growing on me."

"Sounds like your mom made a good choice, then. My mom's boyfriends were assholes."

"That's too bad." It's all I can think of to say. I doubt he wants to supply details.

"How much money did you raise with the speed dating?"

"Seven hundred and fifty-three dollars."

"Kudos."

"Thanks. I thought it was a cool experiment. I did my sociology paper on it."

"Oh, yeah?"

He puts down his latte and leans back against the couch. "So besides organizing speed dating nights for charity, what do you do? I mean, I'm into music, listening and playing, and I'm into art and I wonder what other people do." He's looking at me intently now. "Do you study all the time?"

"Me? Why would you think that?"

"You get really good marks, don't you?"

"They're okay. I study when I have to. Otherwise, I…" I can't tell him my real vocation, can I? Of course not. "I like to hang out with my friends. And I read a lot." Okay, so it isn't the best answer. In fact, it's totally boring. The Oracle would say this *isn't* the way to get a guy fascinated with you. "Oh, and I've started doing some yoga and working out."

"Rodrigo's big on working out. It's like meditation for him. I was thinking of starting to go to the Y."

"Cool, that's where I go." But wait—if he goes he'll realize I'm hardly ever there.

"So what's your workout routine?"

"Uh…" Okay, so maybe I overstated my case. I don't have an actual *routine*. "Well, I'll do a yoga class and then use the treadmill. And maybe some weights afterward." I hope I'm not lying; I hope curling five-pound dumbbells constitutes doing weights.

"Weights, huh? I can see that." He gives my biceps a little squeeze. And suddenly I'm having another mini panic attack, wondering if he's going to kiss me right here and now.

But he's not moving closer. I wonder if he realizes that he's affecting me this way. Probably not, because his hand moves away.

"Do your parents know where you are, Kayla?"

The mention of my parents is like a splash of cold water. "They know I'm—" *On a date.* Thankfully I catch myself in time. "They know I'm out with somebody.

Why?" Does he want to stay out late? Go somewhere exciting? I could call home…

"I was thinking you'd better get back. They wouldn't want you taking the subway too late."

It's only ten! I want to say. But I guess he's right. I should probably be grateful that he's pointing out the time.

"I'll walk you to the subway. You take the Q?"

"Yeah. What about you?"

"The N."

"That's the opposite way."

His mouth curves up at the side. "I know. Let's go."

We get up, put our cups on the counter and step outside into the crisp air. Wishing I wore a heavier jacket, I hug myself against the cold. His clothes are even flimsier than mine, but his jacket is hanging open like the cold doesn't affect him. I bet he likes the breeze flattening his shirt against his chest.

I keep wondering if he's going to put his arm around me or take my hand. I'm close enough that he could do either if he wanted.

He insists on swiping his Metrocard and waiting with me on the platform. I'm grateful, since the station is pretty deserted. It isn't late, but it's a weeknight.

I see the lights of the train pulling up. My heart thunders as I turn to him. "That was fun," I shout over the noise.

"Yeah. Night, Kayla."

Then he turns and walks away.

I step onto the train. As the doors close and the train accelerates, I stand there, dumbfounded.

What just happened? Where the hell is my good-night kiss?

I WAS ROBBED! Robbed, I tell you. When I get home, I go straight to the computer to write a blog.

To Kiss or Not to Kiss?
The Rules of Kissing on the First Date:
A Plea to Guys Everywhere

A lot of fuss has been made over the question, should people kiss on the first date? The answer is not an easy one, but some rules apply.

Body language is very important. If a girl looks likes she wants you to kiss her, then do it. If she seems reserved, then hang back and offer a hug or a kiss on the cheek, letting her know what a great time you had. If you're not interested, don't kiss her at all.

Whatever you do, don't leave her wondering whether or not you're interested in a second date. And please don't leave her wondering whether your night out was, in fact, a date or not…

I'm tempted to leave a copy of the blog in Jared's locker, but of course, I would never do that.

The thing is, we had a great date. But now I have an

awful fear that it wasn't a date at all and that he just sees me as a friend, someone to hang out with. He didn't even *try* to kiss me. And I don't buy that he was trying to be a gentleman. He's a teenage guy!

If anyone but me were involved, the Oracle would have plenty of advice. But it's impossible to be objective when it's my own love life.

I remember that, a few weeks ago, I wrote a blog called *How To Tell If He's Interested In a RELATIONSHIP With You.* I capitalized the word *relationship* because a guy may be attracted to you without being interested in a real relationship, as I discovered with both Case Study No. 1 and 2.

I find the blog and skim it over, looking for words that fit my situation.

...Keep in mind that some people are gushy and immediately want to sweep you off your feet. These people are a lot of fun, but often their interest in you dies quickly. It may be better to find someone whose interest in you increases over time, or who is reserved at the beginning. A cautious person, who will express his feelings only after getting to know you well, is often a safer long-term bet.

This is something, isn't it? By my own advice, his lack of gushiness doesn't necessarily mean there's no relationship potential. I wish I knew!

AT 10:07 THE NEXT NIGHT, I'm sitting in my bedroom stewing in my bad mood thanks to last night's NKF (no kiss fiasco) and the fact that Jared still hasn't called. It doesn't help that the most entertaining part of my night was when a customer bought a jar of Metamucil and a stack of tabloids and whispered, "Bathroom stuff."

Ick!

The only thing that got me through the horrid shift at Eddie's was thinking there would be a phone message waiting for me when I got home. But there was no message, and Mom and Erland confirmed that no one had called.

I feel like an idiot. I really thought he would call. At school today, Jared was warm. Jared was flirty. Jared was even touchy-feely. But it's true, he said nothing about going out again. Come to think of it, he didn't refer to last night at all.

Tanner, my stuffed bear, is looking down at me with a frown. *Yes, Tanner, I know. I'm waiting for a guy to call. It's utterly, totally wrong.*

If Jared doesn't know that he should call me, he's beyond clueless. Even if he's at work, he could give me a quick call on his cell. Calling is a basic courtesy to the person you're dating, a keep-in-touch, just-checking-in mechanism to let the person know you're thinking of them.

If I had his number, which I don't, would I have the courage to call him?

Probably not. There's no point, anyway, because Jared calling (or not calling) will tell me if he's interested in me.

I feel a blog coming on.

To Call or Not to Call: The Rules

It's tense. It's distracting. You jump every time the phone rings.

Since the beginning of the telephone, girls have been wondering whether the guy will call. Sometimes he says he will but never does. Sometimes he doesn't say he will but he does, anyway.

The rule is usually two days. If he doesn't call you within two days of getting your phone number (or within two days of the first date), your future does not look promising. If a guy likes you, he's eager. Sure, he might wait a day not to seem too eager. But if he waits longer than that, it's not a good sign.

If he comes up online, don't instant-message him first. IMing him won't tell you what you need to know: is he interested?

In this day and age, there is no excuse for not calling. If you're very busy, you can send a quick text message or a one-line e-mail. There is always a way.

One of my clients, we'll call her Tara, gets asked for her phone number frequently. Most of the time, the guys do not call. Tara recently tried a new strategy. When she met a cute guy and he asked for her phone number, she said, "I'll take yours instead." By doing this, she figured she could call him whenever she wanted and not wonder whether he'd call.

Allison van Diepen

Two days later, Tara called him. The guy said he was on the other line but he'd call her right back. So she gave him her phone number.

He didn't call back.

The moral of the story is this: There is nothing you can do to avoid the will-he-call-me problem. He will either call or he won't. If he does, that will give you the answer to the most fundamental question of dating: is he interested in me or not?

Good luck, and God bless,
The Oracle

I post the blog and log on as the Oracle. While I was at work I missed three instant messages. That's fifteen bucks lost! Hopefully they'll try again sometime. I really have to quit my job soon. If I'm serious about taking the Oracle to the next level, I need to spend more time in front of the computer.

Bling! Loveless23 has instant-messaged me.

Loveless23: You're not easy to get in touch with, Oracle.
Oracle: I apologize. I am here for you now, Loveless23. How are you doing with the woman in your office?
Loveless23: You remember that?
Oracle: The Oracle remembers all things.

And keeps detailed notes. Ha-ha.

Loveless23: Well, I finally worked up the courage to ask
her out. She said yes. We went out. It was awkward at
first but then it went really well.

Oracle: That's wonderful! Will there be a second date?

Loveless23: I'm not sure. I was hoping she might ask me
out next time.

Oracle: How did the last date end? Did you talk about
another date?

Loveless23: No. It ended pretty fast. I didn't even have a
chance to kiss her. Well, I could have, but I was hoping
she'd make a move. She's confident. She knows who she is.

She knows who she is? Something about that rings a bell...

Oracle: Did you call her?

Loveless23: I'm not sure if I should. We went out last
night. I don't want her to think I'm crowding her or
anything.

Oracle: You have to use your own judgment on that. Did
you get the impression that she likes you?

Loveless23: She's friendly. But she's nice to everyone.
That's just who she is. I don't know if she even realizes
we went on a date. She might think we went out as friends.

Oracle: Maybe that's because you didn't kiss her. If you
had, you'd probably have a good sense of whether she liked
you or not—depending on whether she kissed you back.

Loveless23: I'm starting to regret that I didn't. Especially when I read your blog on that, Oracle. But like I

said, I don't think kissing and calling should only be up to me. This girl's a feminist, she should know that. Anyway, I thought if you like a girl you're *not* supposed to kiss her on the first date.

Oracle: I think that depends on your age group. How old are you?

Loveless23: Seventeen.

Seventeen? I wrote down in my notes that he was twenty-three. Maybe I got confused because of his username.

Oracle: At your age, kissing on the first date is entirely appropriate.

Loveless23: Gotcha. So, Oracle, do you think this girl likes me?

Oracle: That is hard for me to tell. Does she flirt with you?

Loveless23: I'm pretty sure she does. What should I do now? Call her?

Oracle: Yes. The Oracle believes you should call her. She could be hoping for your call right now.

Loveless23: Okay, Oracle. I'll call her. Thanks for your help. Definitely worth the five bucks.

Oracle: Glad to hear it. Good luck, Loveless23.

The phone rings. I almost jump out of my skin. It's the home line. "Hello?"

"Glad you're back in business, Oracle."

I blink. "Uh, what did you say?"

"Am I speaking to the Oracle of Dating?"

"Um. Uh."

"Did I shock you by calling your home line?"

My mind is whirling.

"Jared?"

"You sound really surprised, Kayla. But you wanted me to call, didn't you?"

"Loveless23."

He's laughing. "Yeah, that's me, *Oracle.*"

"How did you know?"

"I didn't figure it out right away. Getting that card in my locker made me wonder if it was somebody at school, and I'd been talking to you right before that. And when the Oracle went off-line, it looked like you were in a bad spot... I still wasn't sure. But when I got home from our date—and, yeah, it definitely *was* a date—and I saw your blog on kissing, I knew. I bet you're blushing right now. I love it when you blush."

Am I ever! I can't believe he knows I'm the Oracle. He knows everything I've been thinking!

"I'll promise you one thing, Kayla. I would've kissed you if I knew you wanted it. And another thing—I won't pass up another chance."

His words take my breath away.

"Are you there?"

"Yeah," I say weakly. "You threw me off. Nobody knows about the Oracle except my sister, one of her friends and Viv."

"I figured that. I won't tell anyone. You can trust me."

"I know."

"The Web site is awesome. Did your sister do it for you?"

"Yeah. How'd you know?"

"You said she was a software engineer. Creating a Web site isn't a big deal for somebody like that. Look, Kayla, I'd really like a second date. And I'm free Saturday night. So if you want to ask me out, feel free."

I laugh. "Let me get this straight. You're asking me to ask you out."

"Right. So will you do it?"

"Okay." I clear my throat. "Will you go out with me Saturday night?"

"Sure. Thought you'd never ask."

fifteen

THE NEXT MORNING IN CLASS our eyes meet. We both smile like we know some secret joke we're not letting anybody in on.

He leans over and whispers, "Morning, Oracle."

I giggle, not just because he knows my identity, but because his cologne is flirting with my senses.

He knows I'm reacting to him, because when he sits down, he's unable to wipe the grin from his mouth.

As the class goes on, I'm thinking of writing a whole new blog on flirting. Flirting without any words at all. With your eyes. With your body. It's amazing how Jared is driving me crazy without really doing anything. And I have the feeling I'm having the same effect on him.

We leave class together and he walks me to the caf, which is in the opposite direction of his next class. When we're about to part, he leans into me. I freeze, wondering if he's coming in for a kiss. But he isn't, he just stands there motionless, so close I'm getting hot all over.

Sweet Lord, I should definitely write a blog on sexual tension!

At the lunch table, my friends are asking a million questions. *Jared? When? Are you sure?* And I answer: *Yes. Now. Definitely.*

AT 3:27 P.M. GERSTAD IS long gone, but she's nice enough to let me stay in the art room as long as I close the door behind me when I leave. She was impressed that I wanted to stay after school on a Friday to finish my project. I didn't tell her I was only staying late because I didn't want to waste my own money buying paints to finish it at home.

I'm standing at my desk, mixing dark blue with white, trying to create a pastel blue like in the photo. A noise makes me look up.

Jared is standing in the doorway.

"Hey. Come see how I'm doing."

He comes up close, peering at the drawing over my shoulder. "Nice job with the background."

"Is this blue right for her dress?"

"Add a bit of yellow… That's it."

"Thanks." Unsure of what to do, I start painting the dress. He's watching me, and he's so close I feel his chest rising and falling an inch from my back. The air around us is charged with electricity.

"I thought you said you had to work," I say.

"I do, in an hour. I just know I won't be able to sleep tonight if I don't take you up on your offer."

"My offer?" My paintbrush is hovering dangerously close to the paper. Jared takes it out of my hand and puts it down.

He turns me around to face him. Oh my God! He's going to do it now!

He takes my face in his hands and kisses me. My knees start to crumble. I close my eyes, clutch his shoulders. His kiss is open-mouthed and hot. It isn't shy, it's electric and demanding. He must have prepped for this—his mouth tastes like peppermint. Oh, God, I hope I don't taste like the spaghetti and garlic toast I had for lunch!

He lets me go too soon. My arms are still locked around his neck. I need him to keep kissing me senseless.

I hug him, and he hugs me back, and I can feel the hard muscles of his arms squeezing me. It feels wonderful. His face is nuzzling my hair. We stand there for several moments before he finally breaks away.

"I couldn't wait, Kayla."

"I'm glad you didn't."

"I'll see you tomorrow night?"

"Definitely."

SATURDAY AFTERNOON, Upper East Side. The hair and nail salons along Second Avenue are full of women getting ready for tonight. I'm meeting Tracey at Darcy's, a cozy living-room-type coffee place à la Central Perk on

Friends. And most important, they have the best chai soy lattes in Manhattan.

I know Tracey's going to freak when she hears about the art-room kiss, AKA the hottest kiss ever! I'm totally pumped to get another one tonight. Or two, or three…

Walking into the café, I head to the spacious room at the back.

I spot Tracey. And she's not alone.

Scott is with her. Their body language tells me everything I need to know.

They haven't seen me yet. Can I make a quick break for the door?

Too late. Scott sees me. He waves me over.

I go up to them and plunk myself on the couch beside Tracey.

"Great to see you," Scott says.

There they are: his ridiculously white teeth. He's definitely getting them bleached. No one who drinks as much coffee as he does has teeth that white.

"Hi." I'm not going to say it's great to see him and I'm sure he knows why. In fact, I'm sure this whole setup is to prove to me that I'm wrong about him (i.e. he really *is* a good guy).

"Let me get you something to drink, Kayla," he says. "Chai soy latte?"

"Okay. No foam." I try to give him a five but he doesn't take it and goes up to the counter.

Tracey turns to me. "I hope you're not mad. Scott really wanted to hang out with you again. He wants to hear all about the Web site."

"You told him about it?"

"Why not? He won't tell anyone that you're behind it."

"I don't like being set up."

"That's not what this is."

"Maybe not. It's more of an ambush."

"I need you to support me, Kayla."

"I support you. I don't support *you and him*. And if you try to convince me there's no *you and him,* I won't believe you."

She sighs. "I won't try to convince you. It's just impor-tant to me that you get along with whoever I'm dating."

"Past behavior is the best indicator of future behavior, Trace. Everybody knows that."

"You can be very judgmental."

"Thanks for the compliment."

Scott is back, putting the drink in front of me. "I've seen your Web site. It's great. How do you know so much about dating? Have you had lots of boyfriends?"

"You don't need to have had lots of boyfriends to give dating advice. You need to learn from the ones you've had." I give Tracey a pointed look.

"So I guess you get some pretty crazy questions, huh?"

"Sometimes." I'm not going to facilitate conversation-making with him. I have a split-second fantasy of grabbing the tea light from under a nearby couple's s'more kit and setting his hair on fire.

Finally Scott gives up, and the conversation moves to work stuff, which is fine with me.

At some point Tracey goes to the bathroom, leaving Scott and me and awkward silence. I decide to lay my cards on the table.

"My sister is a great person."

"Definitely. She's wonderful."

"She deserves someone who's serious and reliable."

"Of course she does. I really care about Tracey."

I look straight into his eyes. "Don't hurt her again."

His eyes widen. I can see he's gotten the message.

It doesn't take a genius.

THAT EVENING, ON THE SUBWAY, I have butterflies in my stomach. I pray that my deodorant is doing its job.

My mind is replaying yesterday's kiss in the art room and I keep wondering a) at what point in the date it will happen again, and b) whether I'll be able to anticipate it in time to pop some gum.

We're meeting at the Forty-second Street subway station right next to the ticket booth. When I arrive, he's already there. We hug a little longer than necessary.

"How about Chevy's?" he says.

"Sure."

We walk outside, craning our necks to look at the Times Square buildings with their ticker tapes and huge fashion billboards. Jared takes my hand as we squeeze through the throngs of people on the sidewalk in front of the New Amsterdam Theatre. I like the strong grip of his hand as he guides me forward.

In the restaurant, the waiter leads us to a booth and gives us menus. We look at each other over the table, smiling like idiots.

"Thanks for coming out," he says.

"I'm the one who asked you, didn't I? I'm glad you didn't have to work."

"I finished a couple hours ago." He toys with a sugar pack. "You know, I've read every blog on your Web site. Gives real insight into that brain of yours."

"Pretty twisted, huh?"

"Nah. I'm just afraid to check the Web site when I get home. If there's a blog called *How to Survive a Bad Date,* I'll know where I stand."

I grin, and he cracks a smile. But I take his point; I'd better be careful not to use my own love life as blogging material. It wouldn't be fair to him.

The waiter comes by and we both order sodas.

"So what'd you do today?" he asks.

"I met my sister for coffee. But when I got there, she

was with her loser ex-boyfriend. He's going to break her heart again, I know it."

"What makes him such a loser?"

"He doesn't know what he wants. He says he loves her one minute, and that he isn't ready for a serious relationship the next. She was on an emotional roller coaster the whole time they were together. He's the type of guy who always feels there's something else out there, something better. He's like my dad. That must be why Tracey's drawn to him."

"That's too bad. I learned a long time ago that you can't tie your happiness to someone else. Your sister's an adult and she's responsible for her own life."

"I know. I'm protective of her, though. I keep feeling like I should be able to prevent her from making mistakes."

"You've got to learn to distance yourself. That's what I had to do with my mom. She's screwed up, I told you that. I can't see her ever being clean. I had to distance myself so that I could stay sane, you know? It's not the same as with your sister, it's a lot more extreme, but you get the point."

"How often do you see your mom?"

"Twice a year. I dread it. I know I should go more—she's only two hours away. But I can't handle it. I talked about it with Rodrigo. He said it's okay if I put myself first, and that's what I'm doing. Anyway, this is heavy talk for Chevy's. So tell me, how'd you become the Oracle of Dating in the first place?"

The waiter has to come back twice because we're too

busy talking to look at our menus. After we discuss the history of the Oracle, Jared tells me all about the youth center where he works. Lately he's run into problems because a few of the kids have been swiping the art supplies. Most of the kids are foster kids, and Jared understands how it feels not to have the things you want. Problem is, if they keep doing it, the art class will be shut down because the center doesn't have the money to keep replenishing supplies.

Eventually two plates of food—chimichangas and fajitas—are put in front of us and the waiter cautions us not to touch the plates because they're very hot. Still, I manage to embarrass myself when I accidentally rest my finger on the side of the plate and yelp. Jared tells me to dip my finger in his glass of ice water, which he won't be drinking because he prefers his Coke.

I have no room for dessert, but when he orders key lime pie and an extra spoon, I can't resist a few bites.

The bill comes, and the waiter puts it right in front of Jared. I grab for it, but Jared's already holding it. "I'm getting this."

"Thanks, but there's no reason you should. I'm a feminist." I dig into my wallet and pull out a twenty, putting it on the table.

Jared's eyes narrow. He probably has no idea how sexy he looks when he's annoyed. "I can pay for a freakin' dinner, Kayla."

"Yeah, but I don't want to set a precedent. I believe in going Dutch."

One side of his mouth turns up. "How about this—you let me pay this time, and we go Dutch in the future?"

"Okay." I put my twenty back in my wallet. "Thanks."

"You're welcome."

We leave Chevy's. Jared takes my hand, and I hope it isn't just because of the crowded sidewalk.

"What do you want to do now?" he asks. "There's an arcade down the street, and a pool hall and a rock 'n' bowl place."

"Let's take a walk and see where we end up."

We head north on Eighth Avenue. It's a perfect night for November—warm enough that we can walk for a while without freezing, and cool enough to give me an excuse to get close to him. As we walk, we occasionally make fun of tourists with fanny packs, or stop to look at street artists' sketches.

We're watching a middle-aged woman being sketched, and I turn to him. "You could do this. You'd be great."

"You think?"

"I *know.*"

We step into a café for hot chocolate and linger there for a while, the conversation flowing from one topic to another. Eventually, we see the streets get crowded, indicating the theaters must have let out. I catch sight of a digital clock on a billboard. "Oh, no!"

"What?"

"It's after eleven. I have to get home." I look around. "The 2 train is a couple of blocks back."

"All right. I can take that train, too."

We double back to the station, wait ten minutes and get on the train. The car is more than half full. Good for safety, bad for privacy. This is not, I realize sadly, the place where Jared will give me another one of those kisses. And in a few stops, I'll get off the train and I'll have to wait days! I don't think I can handle that. Why can't this be a hundred years ago, when I'd probably be married already, not dealing with this kind of frustration? He looks so tempting sitting there beside me, leaning his head against an ad that reads, *Know HIV,* I just want to eat him up.

When my stop comes, he grabs my hand and gets off the train with me. "I'm not in a rush. I'll walk you home."

I'm not going to argue.

On the walk from the station, we're pretty much silent. Both of us have popped gum in the past few minutes. I'm wired with anticipation.

"What are you thinking about?" I ask.

"Brooke. How I have her to thank for this."

"What do you mean?"

He stops and turns to me. We're standing on the sidewalk in the darkness under a tree. "Because she made fun of you for not getting into the bar. That's how I knew you'd showed up. When I thought you hadn't, I figured there was no way you were interested. Why didn't you tell me you tried to get in?"

"I heard you left with Brooke, so I didn't want you to know I'd made the effort to be there. It didn't seem to matter."

"It mattered to me. I was really disappointed when you didn't show. It was the second time I thought something would happen between us, and it didn't."

"The second time? When was the first?"

"Speed dating night. I thought, when you invited me, that you might put yourself in the same game as me as a way of, you know, breaking the ice. Obviously that theory went out the window when I realized you weren't going to be playing."

"I had no idea. It didn't even occur to me to put myself in the same game as you."

"Yeah, well, it was all in my head. But then in class, you were as flirty as ever. And, Kayla, you really do know how to flirt. So I figured you had to be interested, and I thought we might hook up at my show." He chuckles. "And when you didn't show up, there was Brooke. Do you want to know what we did when we left?"

"I'm not sure."

"I think you do. We went to a diner and ate. She's got a real French fry fetish, that one. Then she caught a cab home and I took the subway. It was no big thing for me. But then she started calling. I figured I'd give her a chance.

So, Kayla, tell me something. The blog you did on love-sickness. What inspired it?"

My jaw drops. "I… A lot of things." I should never have posted that blog! I should've left it in the recycle bin on my desktop.

"Don't worry. I know the blogs are exaggerated to make a point. I'm not imagining you're in love with me. Not yet, anyway."

We walk another block in silence. Once we're a few houses from mine, I stop again. "Maybe we should say goodbye here. My mom and stepdad could be peeking out the window."

He grins and puts his arms around me. I sigh with pleasure at the feel of his lips against my cheek. He kisses along the line of my jaw until he finds my lips. I meet his kiss with all the pent-up passion inside me, our tongues touching, our breaths racing.

"I'm totally tempted," he rasps in my ear, "to find a park somewhere."

I laugh, still clinging to him, my nails pressing into the fabric of his shirt under his jacket.

"God, you're so beautiful." He cups my face, brushing strands of hair aside.

I smile and kiss him again. This time the kiss is slower and deeper. Heat surges through me. Our bodies are pressed together so tightly that our chests are rising and falling with the same uneven rhythm.

Our lips pull away, and he's kissing my cheeks and chin hungrily, and I throw my head back and look up at the stars with a dreamy grin.

I feel him inch back a little, though he hasn't let go. "Kayla, it's got to be past midnight… Your parents are going to hate me."

I press my watch light: 12:19 a.m. Mom and Erland aren't sticklers about being home at twelve on the dot, but he's right, I better go in.

We have one last kiss. I can't think of anything to say, but I realize I don't have to. After passion like that, saying I had a great time would seem silly.

AT 1:47 A.M., I'M LYING in bed cursing him. Jared has awakened something in me that won't be put to sleep. I feel like a runner, pumped and ready, waiting for the starting gun to go off. All I can think about is the pressure of his lips on mine, the tongue that tasted like peppermint gum, the way his strong, hard body pressed up against me, the way his arms locked around me…

There is no doubt about it.

I am in lust.

sixteen

"Is HE YOUR BOYFRIEND or what?" It's Monday in the caf and my friends are on my case. Now it's Sharese's turn to bug me. "*I don't know* is no kind of answer!"

Which brings me to a question that many people ask the Oracle: at what point do two people who are dating become a couple?

Is it when one person asks the other to date exclusively, and he or she agrees?

Is it just a matter of two people falling into a couple's routine and no words are necessary?

My friends aren't the only ones wondering if Jared and I are a couple. I'm wondering, too. We talk on the phone every night; even if he's at work he calls to check in. And there's been other boyfriendly behavior. Note-passing in class. Kisses before school, after school and in the hallway between classes. No roses or charms for my bracelet or

Allison van Diepen

anything, but it's only the first week. I'm not the kind of girl that needs that stuff, anyway.

I prefer words. More than any romantic gift or action, it's his words that drive me crazy. Jared thinks I'm beautiful. I know that I'm not. But I believe that *he* believes I am.

I kind of know what he means, because I think he's beautiful, too. He's got the bluest eyes I've ever seen, and the most adorable, crooked smile. Most of all, I think he's *hot*. And hot is not just about height and shoulders and all those things that make Declan McCall the talk of the girls' locker room. Hot is about vibe, about sensuality, about electricity.

And when it comes to electricity, Jared's a freaking power station! Sometimes we'll be working in the art room and he'll give me this smoky look, fully aware of what it's doing to my hormones. Then I'll lick my lips and see his eyes go wide.

Anyway. There's no way I'm going to ask Jared if I'm his girlfriend or not. The Oracle knows that would sound needy. In time, he'll clarify, and until then, I'll play it by ear.

"Jared is definitely your boyfriend," Sharese says. "You don't smooch in the hall with someone you're just seeing."

"Did you say *smooch?*" I have to laugh. "We don't smooch in the hallway, we just kiss now and then. We're both not into PDA. That's so junior high. What about you, Sharese? Are you finally going to do something about Mike P.?"

Sharese looks dejected. "I'm such a loser. Consider Operation Dairy Freez terminated."

"Why give up now?" Ryan asks. "You've been talking about this guy for months!"

"Because I'm living a pipe dream. I don't even know where that expression comes from—what does a pipe have to do with a dream?"

We all shrug.

"I told you—pass him a note with your name and phone number, then take off," Ryan says.

"That's so sixth grade."

"Would it be easier if someone did it for you?" I ask.

"That's even worse. That's *fifth* grade. He's going to think I'm immature."

I shake my head. "If he's interested, he's not going to care how you give him your number, just that you do."

"And if he doesn't contact me?"

"Then it probably means he has a girlfriend," Ryan answers. "You'll move on. And you won't look back and wish you'd done things differently."

Just like how I felt when Jared got together with Brooke. I'd wished I'd acted earlier. I hope Sharese doesn't miss her chance. Even if he doesn't call her, at least she'll know. But she's got to decide this herself.

"Give him the note," Viv says, "unless you're willing to ask him to his face."

"I could never ask him to his face!"

"Ah, no big deal. We all know you never meant to make a move." Ryan is using classic reverse psychology.

Sharese perks up. "That's not true! I meant to make a move. But my stomach feels sick when I even think about it. I could, literally, throw up."

"Please don't," we say in unison.

"Maybe I'm old-school," Sharese admits. "Part of me thinks that he would've asked me out, or slipped me a note, if he felt the same way."

"Why, because he's a guy?" Ryan asks.

"Yeah."

"It's not up to the guy anymore," Viv says.

I nod. "Women who think like that will get left behind. The proactive ones will find men. Especially considering the male-female ratio in New York City."

"You sound like the Oracle of Dating," Ryan says.

Little does he know. "Look, Sharese. Mike P. is not the type of guy to ask you out while he's serving you ice cream. He's way too shy for that. Plus, guys don't tend to premeditate like that. Isn't that right, Ryan?"

"Absolutely."

Sharese straightens. "You're right. I'm going to do it! Sometimes you have to take a chance."

OPERATION DAIRY FREEZ enters its final phase.

I check my watch—7:35 p.m. "You can go in any time, Sharese. He should be at the cash by now."

Amy and I are with her for moral support, which she appears to badly need, because she's asked us about ten times how she looks.

Sharese takes a deep breath. "You're sure I don't have anything on my face?"

Amy laughs. "I told you, you look gorgeous!"

"Absolutely Sharesalicious."

"Thanks, guys. Here goes!"

Sharese gets off the bench, straightens her clothes and heads inside the shop. I look at my watch. This shouldn't take more than a few minutes; we haven't seen anyone go inside in the last while, so we know he's not busy.

"I'm so glad she's finally doing this," Amy says. "I'm sick to death of hearing about this guy."

"I hope it works out. He'd be crazy not to go for her."

"Oh, he'll go for her. No guy would pass up a chance like this unless, well, he has a girlfriend. But I peg him for single."

"How do you know?"

"I can tell. It's a gift. What can I say?"

Sharese steps out of the door, her eyes full of tears.

We rush up to her. "What happened?"

"He's…gone." Her lips barely move.

"What do you mean, he's gone?" Amy asks. "He's not working today?"

"He stopped working there last week. They wouldn't give me a number where I can reach him. I've lost my chance!"

Amy puts an arm around her, guiding her to the bench.

"You didn't necessarily lose your chance. We'll probably spot him working somewhere else."

"Amy's right," I say. "You could easily run into him." But who's to say he didn't get a job in Manhattan? Who knows if he even lives in this neighborhood?

Sharese rubs her eyes, smearing her mascara. "I'm such an idiot. I had months to do something but I was too chicken!"

Amy gives her a little nudge. "Aw, c'mon, don't you believe in fate?"

"Uh, yeah."

"Then you know that if it's meant to be, you'll cross paths again. If you don't run into him, that means the relationship wouldn't have worked out, anyway. Some quiet guys are very possessive, you know."

Sharese looks at her, unsure of whether to be comforted. "You think he would have been abusive?"

"You never know about guys. Sometimes the innocent-looking ones are the worst. I'm just saying. No matter how it works out, it's for the best."

Kudos to Amy—she's damned good at talking B.S.

"Maybe you're right. I should leave it to fate. My mom always says I should put things in God's hands."

I'm not sure we should be bringing God into this, but oh well. I want her to feel better.

I realize that for Sharese, Mike P. will be a love that was never realized. A *what-if* that will always haunt her.

Unless Amy's right about fate. The jury's out on that one.

WHEN I GET HOME, Mom gives me the news. "Tracey called. She's going out of town this weekend so she won't be able to meet you for coffee. She'll be in Connecticut with Scott."

I scowl. "I should've set his hair on fire when I had the chance!"

Mom and Erland exchange an uncomfortable glance.

"You can't stand him, either, Mom. Admit it."

"I'm not his biggest fan. But we have to accept her decision. I *am* interested, however, in hearing about your new boyfriend."

My boyfriend?

Was that the answer all along? Is it when your mom notices that you're dating someone that he becomes your boyfriend?

"You're just trying to change the topic so I won't be upset about Tracey and Scott."

"I would like to meet this Jared," the Swede says.

Mom nods. "Me, too. Should we have him over for dinner next week, Erland?"

"Yes, indeed we should."

Huh? What the hell is going on? "You can't invite him without asking me!"

I picture an uncomfortable dinner in which Jared is served up a smorgasbord of questions on philosophy, theology and current events, followed by Mom's favorite board game, *Hallelujah! The exciting new game that combines Bible facts with fun!*

No, thank you.

"Having him over for dinner is a bit much. I'll ask him to come to the door so you can meet him sometime. You can see what he looks like."

"Tell us about him," Mom says.

"He's a senior. He's an artist and a musician."

"I hope he is not one of those young men I see on the train with those piercings and big boots," the Swede says.

"He's not a goth or an emo kid, if that's what you're thinking. He's going to study visual arts in college."

Erland looks thoughtful. "Perhaps he could be an art teacher. Teachers make a good living, you know."

"You should tell him that, Erland."

"When he comes over for dinner?"

"When you meet him at the door."

Subject: My boyfriend is jealous of my books!

Dear Oracle,

I have the most ridiculous problem. My boyfriend is jealous of my favorite book characters!

I admit, I'm a bookie—you know, like a foodie, but with books. I'm the type of person who talks about book characters like they're real. My bedroom wall is covered in posters of my favorite book characters (I've drawn them myself!). I'm not happy if I'm not reading a book, and I die a thousand deaths with anticipation as I'm waiting for books by my favorite authors to come out. My friends don't understand why I'm like this, but I've got some friends online who feel the same way. Honestly, I love my books so much that I would do anything to make the characters real!

My boyfriend gets annoyed when I go on about my favorite characters, but most of the time he puts up with it. Then yesterday, all that changed. He saw that I have a MySpace account under the name Cassandra, and that I've been chatting with a few guys who have Alejandro accounts. (Alejandro is Cassandra's vampire lover in the book *Eternity*— hottest couple EVER!) Now, it's true, I was chatting with these guys in a pretty romantic way, but it was just role-playing. Well, my boyfriend freaked out. He called it cheating! He wants me to close down the account and stop chatting with my Alejandros.

My boyfriend is being such a control freak. What can I do to get him to chill out?

Help me!

Cassandra

I forward the e-mail to Jared. It's always good to have a second opinion, and a male perspective doesn't hurt, either.

A few minutes later, he calls me. Before I can even say hi, he says, "That girl's a nut job."

"I know a few people who like role-playing. I hear it's fun."

"This is what you'd call emotional infidelity, Oracle. He should dump her on her ass."

I smile to myself. *Emotional infidelity* isn't a term you'd expect from a teenage guy. But then, I use it fairly often, and he's obviously been reading my Web site for a while. "Yeah, it's crazy that she thinks he shouldn't have a problem with it."

"Let me reply to this one," Jared says.

"No way. You're a little too, er, blunt for this business."

"I would just tell her the truth—that she should get her nose out of a book and into real life, and look for a guy in real life who turns her on. Obviously the guy she's dating right now isn't doing it for her."

"I don't think it means she's not into her boyfriend. It's just that she also likes to fantasize about other guys."

"Right, guys who *aren't real*. Look, she hasn't been married to the guy for twenty years or anything. She should be fantasizing about her boyfriend. And if she isn't, there's a problem."

"You have a point there."

"Think about it. Who do you fantasize about, Kayla? No wait, don't answer that."

"Why not? I fantasize about you."

"Yeah, me, too. About you, I mean."

Dear Cassandra,

There is nothing wrong with being swept into the world of a book and being mesmerized by its characters. But if your obsession with these characters is negatively affecting your personal relationships and preventing you from being present in your own life, then there is a problem.

I don't think anyone would blame your boyfriend for feeling the way he does. Having "pretty romantic" conversations with other guys, whether it involves role-playing or not, would make most boyfriends uncomfortable. My guess is that his freak-out was not just about that one issue. I think it stemmed from knowing that these characters play such a central role in your life. The online role-playing might've been the last straw.

It's time to put some distance between you and the characters you love. You don't want to look back on your life and see that it was spent in a dreamworld. Make your real life more interesting so that you won't want to trade it for a fictional one. You can do it!

Sincerely,

The Oracle

THE NEXT DAY Gerstad hands back our projects. My hands quiver as I open the cover. Jared is looking over my shoulder.

A-.

I squeal and give Jared a hug. I can't believe Gerstad was so generous! Maybe she realized it was the best I could do considering I have no artistic talent.

She gives Jared back his project. He opens the cover, looks in and nods. I'm not quick enough to glimpse the grade.

"What'd you get?"

"I did well."

"Are you going to show me or not?"

"If you want." He shows me that it's an A+.

"Awesome! You deserve it. If you'd gotten any less than that, I would've staged a protest."

I can hardly wait until after school when we're going for coffee. When the bell rings at the end of class, Jared takes a note out of his bag. "I wrote something for you."

"What is it?"

"You'll see. Just don't get caught reading it in class. See you out front at three-fifteen."

"I'll be there."

I give him a kiss and hurry to my next class. As I sit there, the note is burning a hole in my pocket. And yet I can't take it out. Not only did Jared warn me, but Mr. Werner is notorious for confiscating notes and reading them out loud.

So I ask for the bathroom pass and once there, I open the note, which is covered with Jared's artful doodles.

Dear Kayla,

It's 2:00 a.m. and I should be asleep, but I keep thinking about you. I played back your messages just to hear your voice. Your voice is warm and husky and downright sexy. I remember everything you've whispered in my ear.

Every time I kissed you, every time I touched you, is another event I replay over and over in my mind. Sometimes, when your warm lips touch mine in the hallway, I picture myself grabbing you and pulling you into some deserted broom closet. From there, my imagination runs wild. I'm pressing you against a wall. Your hands tangle in my hair. Your eyes are closed and your lips are full and sweet. I'm amazed at how passionate you are, Kayla. The first time we kissed I felt like I was scorched. And since then all I can think about is getting close to you again…

The note is practically going up in flames in my trembling hands. My body is going into overdrive and I'm standing in the stinking bathroom!

Wait a minute. Does he expect…? What *does* he expect?

A wave of fear chases away some of my excitement. Does he think that because I'm so passionate and I call myself a dating expert that I'm also a *sexpert?*

I'm a minister's daughter, for God's sake! He doesn't think… Does he think I'm not a virgin?

Is *he* not a virgin?

My mind is spinning out of control.

I stuff the note into my pocket and go back to class. I can't pay attention to the lesson because I'm afraid Jared thinks I'm some sort of sex bomb. I mean, I'm sure I will be someday, but not *now*.

It's my fault. I admitted to him last night that I fantasize about him. But that doesn't mean I'm ready to close the deal!

Has Jared already filled his bedroom with candles and rose petals? Has he already visited the drug store?

No, no, no! This is going too fast! I need to talk to him before it's too late.

WHEN I WALK OUT THE front doors, he's waiting for me. "So?" He reaches out to grab my hips and drag me close to him. "Did you like the note?"

"Uh…" I take his hand. "Let's walk."

We head toward the subway station. It's garbage day and the truck hasn't come around yet. I'm trying not to breathe in.

"Easy." He gives my hand a tug so I'll slow down. "Kayla, I'm sorry. I didn't mean to offend you. I thought you'd like it."

"I did. It's just…"

"What?"

I stop walking and turn to him. "I don't want you to

have expectations…in that area. Girls call the Oracle all the time wishing they hadn't done it. I don't want to make that mistake."

Jared stares at me. My heart drops. I wonder if this is it. He's going to dump me on the spot.

Then his lips twitch, giving way to a grin. "I knew I should have put a disclaimer."

"What?

"The note is a fantasy, that's all. I know you're a virgin. How far we go is up to you."

I sigh with relief. "I'm so glad you said that. The truth is, I loved the note. It really turned me on. But I didn't want you to think, you know, that I'll do whatever you want."

"If I were looking for that sort of girlfriend, I wouldn't be with you. That would be stupid."

Girlfriend? Am I his girlfriend?

Yes!

He squeezes my hand. "You can trust me."

Jared is the most wonderful guy ever.

Totally relaxed now, we start walking again. A thought occurs to me. "Wait a minute—why'd you assume I was a virgin?"

Jared smiles and shakes his head.

AN HOUR LATER, I'm stirring my soy mocha-frappa-whatever, enjoying its sweet taste, but paying far more attention to Jared's hand on my thigh.

"How's business?" he asks.

"The Web site's getting more than a hundred hits a day. I'm hoping that by the New Year, I won't have to work at Eddie's anymore."

"The Oracle could be the next big thing. You could be supporting your parents with the profits. You could be supporting me. I've always wanted a sugar mama."

"I'll give you all the bling you want, honey. I could be your patron."

"Brilliant idea."

We both laugh. I sip my drink, thinking of how much I love being with Jared, and how at this moment I feel utterly, supremely happy.

"What are you thinking?" Jared asks.

"That I'm happy to be here."

"Here on earth, or here with me?"

"Here with you. And on earth, I suppose. But mainly with you."

He laughs, then kisses me softly. "Want to know what I'm thinking?"

"Yeah."

"I knew right away that you were somebody I wanted to be close to. There was something different about you. It's like…you know who you are."

I smile. I really am his Girl #13, the one he wanted all along.

seventeen

On Balancing Time Between Friends and Boyfriends

There are some things that are so obvious that the Oracle shouldn't have to write about them. Nevertheless, the Oracle sees the same disturbing trends year after year—people ditching their friends for their new love interest!

This is a MISTAKE for several reasons. The first reason? Unless you marry the person you're dating right now, your relationship will eventually end. When that happens, you will have no friends left! Certainly no friends when you need a shoulder to cry on.

But there are other reasons, too.

If you ditch your friends, you are—whether you like it or not—giving your boyfriend a dangerous message: that he is your priority. You are acting like he is so special that you're willing to trade in years of friendship for him. This can backfire! He might a) feel like you're too clingy and pull away from you, or b) feel like he's in control of the relationship because he knows that you don't have a social life without him.

Making sure that you do right by your friends is especially important for teens. You are not going to get married anytime soon, so why act like it?

How can you balance friendship with romance? Here are three suggestions:

1) Friday and Saturday nights are prized territory. Divide them equally between your friends and your boyfriend—yes, that means one night each!

2) Bring your boyfriend, on occasion, when you're going out with your friends.

3) It's natural that your friends will feel a little upset when they notice that you're spending less time with them. Let them know how much they mean to you. Keep calling them!

"HEY, TRACE," I SAY into the phone. "How was Connecticut?"

"Fine. Scott and I broke up. Could you come over?"

"I'll leave right now."

I grab my jacket and jog to the station. It's Sunday so I have to wait twenty freaking minutes for the train.

What happened between her and Scott? Who broke up

with whom? Is she crushed? If Scott played her again, I'm going to hire someone to break his kneecaps.

When I get off the subway, I jog the two blocks to the high-rise where she lives. I hope she's not going to be bawling when I get there. She's cried so much over Scott, I can't bear to see it again.

Tracey buzzes me into the building and I take the elevator up to the sixth floor. When she opens the door, she looks fragile. We hug.

"Thanks for coming."

Tracey's apartment is the epitome of homey. Since heating is included in the cost of her rent, she keeps it warm and toasty. She bought most of her furniture when she was in college, so the beige couches are worn and covered with mismatched pillows, and the decorations consist of a few knickknacks from her world travels. There's also the hint of a techie in here—the binary clock in the living room, complete with colorful dots that supposedly tell you the time, and the computer with two flat screens in the corner of her living room.

"Want some tea?"

"I'd love it." I follow her into the kitchen, where she fills up the kettle.

"I broke up with him last night and caught a bus back from Connecticut." She drops two bags of orange pekoe into a pot. "He didn't do anything to provoke my decision. We had dinner with his parents Friday night, and they were as sweet as ever. It was so strange, like nothing had changed, like a time warp to a year ago. Except *I'm* not the same person I was a year ago. And it hit me—what am I doing with him again?"

We go into the living room and sit down on the couch. There's a bag of chips next to me. I grab a few.

"He was shocked. I think he actually wanted to give it a shot this time. It might've worked for a while. I told him we just didn't fit. But the truth is, being with Scott is pure masochism." She digs into the bag and pulls out some chips. "I don't know how I let myself get sucked in again after all he put me through."

"Healing the wounds of the past. I think sometimes when you're attached to someone and they hurt you, you want to go back to them to heal yourself of that hurt. It never works, though."

"It's weird. Even though logically I knew it was a bad idea, there was something compelling about him—like a drug. You know what I mean?"

I nod. *Do I ever.*

"I wish I'd listened to you, *Oracle*. How'd you get so wise?"

I have to laugh. "Trial and error. I don't always give good advice."

"You're being modest. Anyway, I know I did the right thing. But I still feel bad."

"Because you hurt him?"

"No, definitely not that. I know Scott, and he'll hit the ground running. It's just, coming home to this empty apartment…reminds me of how nothing ever works out."

"It only has to work out once, Trace."

"I know. It's all so strange. I meet a lot of guys that seem to have potential, and then I realize they're not what I thought." She turns to me. "I'm starting to think I'm the problem, not them."

"You? Don't you dare turn this on yourself, Trace. You're the most amazing woman ever—those guys are the weird ones, not you!"

She cracks a smile. "Thanks. I just mean that my judgment isn't always the best. Okay, sometimes it's downright stupid. I get infatuated with guys quickly, and when I find out what they're really like, I'm disappointed. It's a vicious cycle, and I'm tired of it."

I give a supportive nod. She's right, and I'm glad she's finally realizing it.

"Maybe I'll become a nun, devote myself to God's work." She trades in the chips for some brownies—freshly made, I note.

"We're not Catholic. And you don't need to be a nun to do that—hello, our mom?"

"Good point. But I really do need a break from dating. I need to think of a better game plan than I've had to this point."

A break from dating? *Now?* But what about Rodrigo? How are they going to fall in love?

"Actually, there's this guy I'd like to set you up with, Trace. From what I hear, he's fantastic."

Tracey shakes her head. "That's really nice of you to try to find someone for me, but I'm not ready. I've dated too many guys in the past few months, and I need to take a step back and figure out what I want."

My sister is being wise. I can't fault her on that. It's what I've always wanted her to do: think before she acts.

"So what's he like?" she asks.

I grin. Despite her romantic trouble, Tracey is still Tracey.

"To Viv!" Ryan holds a slice of pizza in the air. "Now that Viv has rejoined the world of the living, may she have many wild times!"

"To Viv!" we all echo, lifting our slices and touching the tips together before taking bites. Amy's bite ends up ripping the entire top of her pizza off, and the whole cheese-pepperoni surface dangles from her mouth. She gives a pizza-filled laugh while grabbing the hot stringy cheese with her hand. We're all in stitches watching her.

We knew we'd have to do something fun to celebrate the end of Viv's grounding, but she warned us that we shouldn't do anything that could get her into further trouble. So we decided to play it safe and go out for pizza and pool at a sports bar called Maclaren's.

Jared is sitting across the booth from me, his jaw working as he eats his pizza. God, he's so beautiful. I keep having to remind myself that he's really here, that he's really my boyfriend. Tonight marks his first official outing with my friends.

As I watch everyone interact, I wonder what it would be like for a newcomer to go out with my friends. The conversation is fast-paced and jumps from one topic to another. There's lots of talk about celebrity gossip and crazy teachers and random trivia, with occasional political rants. I hope Jared doesn't think my friends are shallow, because they're really not—they just like to talk about silly things sometimes.

I have to admit, though, that my friends do gossip a lot. And when Ryan starts on the topic of Brooke, I feel myself tense. I wish he had the sense not to mention her with Jared around.

"She and Declan were spotted making out at Kirsten's party Saturday night. They're not official yet, but it's only a matter of time."

"I finally found out why their first breakup was so traumatic for her," Amy says. "Apparently he slept with one of her friends at a party while Brooke was downstairs. That was his way of letting her know he was moving on."

Jared hadn't told me the details of why Declan was such a jerk, and I sensed it was to protect Brooke's privacy. But I guess word had finally gotten out.

"Makes you look like Prince Charming," Ryan says to Jared, who smirks. My friends know that the story circulating about why Jared and Brooke broke up isn't exactly the real deal. I had to convince them of that, or they would've used any means necessary to stop me from dating him.

I look around at my friends, thinking how good it is that we look out for one another.

AFTER SCHOOL THE NEXT DAY, Jared says, "Let's go to my place. I figure it's about time I showed you where I live. And Gina's been bugging me to have you over."

After a few stops on the Q and a transfer to the N, we're in Jared's neighborhood, Bensonhurst. He looks totally at ease on these streets. Something in his movement has relaxed.

"Nice neighborhood." The houses have front porches from the days when people weren't afraid of their neighbors or drive-bys. I can tell this is an old people's neighborhood judging by the people walking by—slowly.

"Yeah, I'm happy here. It's way better than Sunset Park, where I used to live."

He's talking about safety, not scenery.

"Here it is." It's a cute white house that resembles a life-size dollhouse. Jared opens the door. "Gina? We've got a visitor."

He takes off his shoes and I do the same. We find Gina curled up on the living-room couch watching a soap

opera. She's wearing a frilly pink housecoat. Nicely pedi-
cured toes peek out. She mutes the TV.

"Bella Michaela!" She says my name like a true Italian.
Mi-ki-ela.

Gina is surprisingly swift on her feet. She's up off the
couch and in front of me, reaching up to take my face in
her hands, kissing both of my cheeks.

"Such beautiful skin! Come, let's have a snack. I have
cannolis. Do you like cannolis?"

Around the kitchen table, we chat about school and the
neighborhood, which Gina has lived in since the sixties.
I love the way she and Jared get along. I tell her a few
things about myself and my family. She's such a sweet lady.
It's hard to believe she sells lingerie to transvestites. She
seems so innocent.

Suddenly Gina slaps her forehead. "Oh, my, I have a
customer coming in five minutes. I need to set up!"

"Can we help?" I offer.

"Not without permission from your parents." She
winks and scurries out of the room.

Wordlessly, Jared takes my hand and leads me upstairs.

This room is very Jared. Artwork is splashed over the
walls, along with small stars which I guess glow in the dark.
A desk with a computer is by the window.

"You've got a great setup here. Gina's a sweetheart."

"Isn't she?" He plunks down on his unmade bed.

I sit down beside him. "How long were you with your last foster family?"

"A year."

"Were they horrible to you?"

His mouth lifts at the corner. "I don't have a *Good Will Hunting* story. None of my foster parents put out cigarettes on me. That doesn't mean we got along. The last family made it clear that they didn't take me for any reason but the money. I was supposed to get an allowance but they refused to give it to me—said I ate too much of their food, which wasn't true. So I told Rodrigo about it, and he let me stay with him for a couple of months before he found me this place."

"I'm glad you're happy here."

"Me, too. Gina gives me a good allowance from the money she gets. And I help her out by doing repairs, taking out the trash, that kind of stuff."

"Does she have any children?"

"She's got a son who lives on Staten Island. He doesn't come over often, and when he does, he just criticizes. I overheard them arguing because he said she was stupid to let a *street kid* into her house. She said that if I ever decide to rob her, she'd get new furniture with the insurance money."

The doorbell rings so loud I almost jump off the mattress. Jared looks at me apologetically. "Sorry it's so loud. Gina's kind of deaf. Want to listen in?"

"We shouldn't, should we?"

"I don't think it'll do any harm. We won't be able to see the guy's face and he won't see us."

"All right, then."

He takes my hand and we pad into the hallway and halfway down the stairs. We hear them talking in the living room.

"You don't have those kinky boots, Madam Gina?" the gravelly male voice asks. "It clearly says in the ad—"

"I'm-a sorry but I just sold my last pair, Mr. Jones." Gina plays up her accent like she's Italian born. "But I'm-a sure I can interest you in some of my other stock. Just-a take a look at this beautiful lace garter belt. It is special-ordered from Italia."

"It's quite nice."

"At thirty dollars, it's a very good price. In fact, I like you, I'll-a give it to you for twenty-five. You won't find it at any Manhattan boutique."

"Hmm…"

"I also have-a these gorgeous fishnets."

My chest is pumping with repressed laughter. I glance at Jared, who bites his lip and squeezes his eyes shut. We're seconds from bursting.

He yanks my hand and we hurry back up the stairs to his bedroom. He closes the door, flicking on his stereo. Then he bursts, and I burst, and we collapse on the bed.

Jared's laughing so hard he's crying. "Oh, God. That almost killed me. Gina would've never forgiven me if we'd lost it. Her client would've run out."

And then, because he looks so cute, I lean down and gently brush my lips against his. I feel his lips spread in a smile, and then he kisses me back, slow and gentle.

"I'm glad you're here, Kayla."

"Me, too."

I lie back on the bed, and he leans over me, and we kiss again. I see that one of the buttons on his shirt is undone, and my hand creeps into a patch of chest hair. I can't resist giving a little tug.

"Ouch!" he mutters. "You did that on purpose!"

"Um, I'm sorry…"

"Whatever turns you on." He laughs, his warm breath rippling against my neck.

I smile. One kiss melts into another, and my soul is filled with bliss. Jared and I are together at last. And I have to wonder: is this my happily ever after?

The Oracle side of me wouldn't bet on it.

But the romantic in me says, absolutely!

★ ★ ★ ★ ★

Don't miss out on what happens next!
Come back later for the Oracle's next chapter
THE ORACLE REBOUNDS
November 2010

Mara Purnhagen

Kate is confused when she arrives at Cleary High to find the building's been "tagged" with a life-size graffiti mural, and her friend Eli has gone missing....

Available now wherever books are sold!

HARLEQUIN
TEEN

New York Times bestselling author

RACHEL VINCENT

My Soul To Take

SOMETHING IS WRONG
WITH KAYLEE CAVANAUGH
SHE DOESN'T SEE DEAD PEOPLE, BUT...

She senses when someone near her is about to die.
And when that happens, a force beyond her control
compels her to scream bloody murder. Literally.

Kaylee just wants to enjoy having caught the attention
of the hottest guy in school. But a normal date is hard
to come by when Nash seems to know more about her
need to scream than she does. And when classmates
start dropping dead for no apparent reason, only
Kaylee knows who'll be next....

SOUL SCREAMERS

THE LAST THING YOU HEAR BEFORE YOU DIE

*Look for Book 1 in the Soul Screamers series
Available now wherever books are sold!*

HARLEQUIN TEEN

HT003TRR